Generations

Generations

Peter Bowes

For Angie

Bennison Books
A good book is a blessing

Bennison Books Fiction
ISBN: 978-0-9954302-2-8

Contents

Introduction

Generations is the final volume in Peter Bowes' trilogy of essays and stories, the first two being *Bloodlines* (2013) and *Lineage* (2015).

Bowes continues to entertain, move and surprise us with his subtly acute observations of life in all its manifestations. His writing is often at its most affecting when documenting the lives of those who otherwise come and go as we pass them by with barely a second glance.

As Marcel Proust wrote, 'the real voyage of discovery consists not in seeking new landscapes, but in having new eyes'. Bowes gives us those new eyes as we learn to see the world in a different way, a more kindly way, perhaps.

Here, we meet the 'woman by the side of the road', her home a dilapidated caravan, tormented by nighttime noises and cars pulling up outside to terrorise her while she tries to sleep; Ronnie, the alcoholic 'been a single bloke all me life'; and an unnamed man turning up for a reunion but finding no 'special old friend because there was no special young friend forty-five years ago'.

Some of these pieces are haunting, staying in the mind long after reading: Noah, who's 'about eight and lights up a smile every time he sees you looking at him'; and the child Yukio S who 'survived the titanic waves of radiation that cleansed his neighbourhood after the American bomb swept Hiroshima away'. As Bowes observes, 'the melancholy among us'.

However, the author is no less skilled at making us laugh as well as appreciating the simple joys and satisfactions of friendship and shared experiences: the delivery of dog food to an Italian restaurant causes unforeseen chaos in 'The Best Food Available', while in another piece, an overheard conversation about a man with three thumbs takes on a life of its own.

Bowes introduces us to his friends, neighbours and acquaintances with economy, insight and warmth: his best man whom he enjoys gently teasing at a get-together; a neighbour plagued by wild dogs; and a trip to a shoe store made by his wife and daughter with its doubly shocking discoveries.

We also return with the author to his days as a slaughterman in the 'killing rooms', continuing on from the powerful memoirs related in *Bloodlines*, and share painful memories of an outward bound course he attended in his youth that ended in tragedy.

Proust also wrote that the supreme truth of life resides in art. Peter Bowes writes from the heart and captures some of these truths in a style that is uniquely his own. Our world gets a little bigger when we read his work, our empathy and understanding a little broader.

D. Bennison 2017

About the Author

Sent to boarding school aged seven/taught to box by the nuns/buggered off out of a bathroom window after two years/educated rather nicely at Waverley College/terminated early and without a ticket (a few problems with the brothers – nothing life-threatening)/continued the walk to life at Hawkesbury River and Tallangatta outward bound/buried five students and two instructors who drowned in the weir in winter/met the Duke of Edinburgh at a boat handover – strange old fellow him/travelled south with the itinerant fruit pickers/travelled north to Noosa with a few friends who had spare seats in their cars/drove past Lennox without looking/met Bob Cooper, Bob McTavish and Russell Hughes, full of themselves even then, except Bob/1963 grounded in Byron with only Queenslanders as friends/didn't buy any cheap land at Wategos/found work and the meaning of life at Walkers Slaughterhouse/bagged a seat in J Keevers' red Merc.

1964 got on a ship and sailed away forever/landed in the UK in winter/found the Poms a little moody, the girls though were a different matter completely/ challenged a Pom to put me in hospital in a street fight and never saw the bottle/did some of Europe in the back of a car with two Canadians who didn't talk to me/found that Portugal had a few waves/found Tangiers was full of quality kief and extremely cheap rooms and the whiff of Burroughs and Kerouac was still strong/got off a ferry at Gibraltar/stayed a year, took certain liberties/just avoided being belted by UK marines on leave from Biafra/found out that many Moroccan men are 'hands-on' friends, sweet as/got on a ship and went to the US forever/bought a wreck in NJ and went to Mexico via Florida along some very strange roads/met a black lady in Phoenix who thought Australians ate Aboriginals/found waves in Mexico/had our boards tossed off a cliff and shat upon in Baja/figured yanks for dimwits/ washed up in a Vancouver motel in winter with $54 and two books by Steinbeck/sat in a train for four days from Vancouver to Quebec with a young bloke who looked like Dylan/flew back to Gibraltar for the dark-haired girl/introduced Bob Dylan as ambient music in a couple of nightclubs/brought the dark-haired girl home to Bondi/worked in enough Sydney pubs to learn how to duck a fight and land a punch/two daughters joined us after a while and they still insist on their supremacy/washed cars/wired up old river mansions/worked in bars, nightclubs, building sites, slaughterhouses, hotels, farms, orchards, car-yards, game boats, nightclubs, river boats, offices.

Potted surfing history: Bondi in the 50s/Byron in the 60s/northern beaches in the 70s to '10/back of Byron today – friend of some better side of human nature.

PB

Part One
Stranger than Fiction

Debbie Come by Lately
Up This Way

T he Northern Rivers

Imagine

Thirty-six inches of rain in two days … all the roads cut, creeks overflowing, bridges down, no power, eighty knot wind gusts. Debbie was a big one. Flood water levels still rising, people missing in the hills, homes washed away, cattle drowned. Fences down, dogs loose, seas apocalyptic, beaches ravaged, centuries old trees uprooted, culverts jammed with debris and carcasses, rivers thick, brown and fast. Hundreds of shops and homes inundated, snakes on the roof. Farms abandoned, thousands of acres of water where grazing lands once were. Horses dead, entangled in barbed wire.

An old woman living alone in a house with water up to her knees, no phone, no near neighbours. She's eighty-five. If she leaves the house she will be swept away, if she stays inside she will drown, if she climbs the roof she will fall. Three days now.

What else is there to do but sit in the dark and cast about for a suitable subject to write about when the Internet flicks back on. Something to ease the tension of the past few days. Did I say the rum ration was depleted? The booze cupboard bare? The refrigerator coloured with mould and full of ruined food? No dry matches?

Only five candles left.

Mould.

It's in every drawer, every wardrobe; all the clothes are damp, the bedsheets and blankets. Mosquitoes whine in and out of the doors and windows, dozens of small cockroaches crowd the walls at night. No power for the water pump, ergo no showers, a puddle of muddy water in the sink. Everything festering in the damp. Somebody in the house coughing incessantly, someone else sneezing. Both dogs have disappeared. There's a litter of wren nests under the wall, the crows are out. And a pale goshawk, flying like a ghost.

Shoes

I have a daughter who likes shoes. It's a woman thing and my fair wife is a party to the condition.

They both walked into a shop in Bangalow today; a hinterland hamlet, a little quieter than usual with so many excited locals down in Sydney for the Mardi Gras.

A pair of leopard skin slip-ons for sale, female variety, were available at the bargain price of $350. And on the bottom of the sole was a little sticker that said the skins were peeled off farmed leopards. Hand-reared farmed leopards.

They also had a pic of farmer Bill the leopard man on a window poster, he was all smiles and goodwill. This product was moving in Bangalow.

Problem with old Bill was that he had no hands.

No worries, said Bill, further down on the poster. With leopards, shit happens.

The Man with Three Thumbs

The small whiteboard above Les Aitken's bed read 'Nil by mouth' – and Les did not look so good. He was lying on his back with one eye closed and his mouth gaping open. His skull was bandaged and his knuckles looked as if they'd been scraped along a brick wall. His bottom lip was pouched out and livid. A laceration on his cheek was sutured with fine black thread and coloured a vivid yellow. One of his legs was raised on pulleys and his thigh was heavily bandaged. The exposed bare foot was still caked with gore.

Les's oily black hair was pigtailed tight across his skull and roughly inked prison tattoos covered all his exposed upper arms. Some of his teeth were missing. He had the look of a man well used to the hard life.

'I reckon he's done his ribs in meself,' said old Eric with a low cackle, 'he was coughin' up somethin' terrible last night.'

John from the St Vincent de Paul society nodded and looked out the window. It was the third Sunday of the month and his turn to visit the wards. It was wet and cold.

Eric sat up very slowly and beckoned John closer. He looked over at the other beds in the ward and then winked slyly.

'The coppers brought him in late last night and stayed until the quack knocked him out with a needle. And you know what I heard 'em sayin?'

'What's that?'

'The bloke's got three thumbs.'

'Can't be done.'

'That's what they bloody said, so help me!'

'Who?'

Eric gave an exasperated sigh and levelled a pitying look at John.

'The bloody coppers! How about listenin' to a man for a change. I heard 'em say he was the only bloke that they had ever collared who had three of 'em.'

'Thumbs?'

'My oath! I'm waitin' for him to wake up and scratch himself or sumthin.'

John looked over at the injured man lying asleep in the next bed but could only see one hand. And that was clenched.

'Must be rough shakin' hands with him,' said Eric, and with another low chuckle sank deep into his pillows.

Les's mother had been called by the hospital at eight-thirty that morning. Her son was in no danger but they suggested she make her way over as soon as possible. They didn't mention he'd been escorted into casualty not long after midnight by two policemen who were coming back at midday to interview him.

Mrs Aitken stood at the entrance to the bus shelter only just managing to keep out of the rain. A steady southerly blew in from the sea and she knew from long experience that the three youths sprawled over the one sheltered seat would not move for their own mothers, let alone her.

So she stood with her back to them and worried about her boy, Les. What now?

'Mr Aitken! Mr Les Aitken!'

Curtain screens had been drawn around Les Aitken's bed and the two policemen and doctor standing beside it. In the next bed, Eric lay tense and silent, his eyes as bright as a sparrow's, his ears straining to hear every word.

'Are you Mr Les Aitken of 15 Bidura Crescent Eden?'

'Yeah.'

'Do you remember being brought in here at about twelve forty-five last night?'

'Nuh.'

'Do you recollect your whereabouts yesterday evening?'

'Say what?'

'Do you have any recollection of the places you may have visited yesterday evening?'

'Where was yer drinkin' yesterday, Les?' This from the senior constable who until then had been silent.

There was a pause as Les broke into a coughing spasm. When he stopped he groaned.

'Well?'

'Plenty of places, one of the blokes had won a packet at the races and we was helpin' him spend it.'

'What bloke?'

'Mate of Spotter's, don't know 'im meself, but he had it in bundles.'

Eric drank it all in, waiting for the conversation to turn to the thumbs.

Downstairs, Mrs Aitken stood at the hospital's front desk waiting for the receptionist to look up. The long walk from the bus stop to the hospital in steady rain had saturated her. Her thin hair was plastered flat onto her skull and she knew that the small catch in the back of her throat was the precursor to another dose of the chills.

She waited.

Eric leaned far out from his bed as he heard the rustle of an envelope being opened and shaken out, the rattle of small change emptied onto Aitkin's bedside table.

'This is of particular interest to us, Mr Aitken, and we would appreciate an explanation.'

The ward doctor moved quickly to assist as Les attempted to sit up while the two officers watched motionless. Eric fell out of his bed with a clatter, dragging his sheets with him.

Later that day, Mrs Aitken took the bus home. She was still damp from the morning's downpour and sneezing intermittently.

She would have a hot bath, then make a pot of tea and count the money the police had given to her for safekeeping before she left the hospital. The money they had found in her son's pocket.

She reckoned there was about three thousand dollars in her handbag. The police had offered to drive her home but Mrs Aitken did not accept favours from any man.

At about the same time, Eric and John were sitting in the television room watching as Les rolled his cigarette, waiting for him to resume his story. A few illicit cans of beer stood behind their feet.

'The boofhead would bet on anythin',' Les continued through the blue smoke. 'There we was standin' in the bar havin' a quiet drink and the silly bugger's bettin' on how many rings are on me glass after I've finished it.

'For a hundred bucks, he says five. I say four without lookin' and I take it off him. Easy.'

Old Eric cackled with delight.

John had to ask.

'How did you know there were only four rings on your glass?'

'Mate, I always only take four to finish a schooner, ever since I was a kid. Anyway, then he wants to go double or nothin' on just about anythin' in the room and he couldn't throw a dart to save his life. We ended up throwing double anything for fifty bucks a time and he was doin' his money cold every throw, plus he was pissed.

'The bloke was dead set nuts. Then when he realised that I'd ended up with about half his wad he went the whole Muhammad Ali on me.'

A nursing sister walked by and the three men shifted their beer cans further out of sight. Eric chortled softly as she disappeared back into the ward.

Les picked up his beer and took a long and appreciative pull at it. Exhaled contentedly.

'There's no such thing as a bad beer.'

Or a good job,' said Eric.

Eric volunteered to push Les back to the ward and John set off in search of his offsider from Vinnies, eventually finding him on the patient's verandah, drinking coffee.

Larry sat mostly silent as John retold the tale.

'… Les's problems started when Spotter's mate decided that he wanted all his money back and turned animal. Poor old Les copped a fair hiding.'

'And the thumb?'

'Spotter's mate thought he'd finished Les off and started to go through his pockets to get the money, but Les still had some gumption left and grabbed him.

'They knocked over a table and landed on the broken glasses. The bloke still had his hand in Les's pocket and his thumb was clean sliced off by the same piece of glass that punctured Les's thigh.

'Then the publican showed up with the coppers, Spotter's mate was coshed and someone called for an ambulance.

'The police found the thumb along with the money when they searched Les at the hospital.'

Mrs Aitken picked up the brass-framed photo of her only son Leslie and held it up to her bedside light. The boy was wearing a pair of oversized swimming trunks and holding a gushing hose over his head. Behind him on a clothesline a large pair of overalls ballooned in the breeze.

He had a huge grin on his face and was shouting something at her. She had forgotten what.

He had always been a good boy.

The Best Food Available

Elio Fragganzi and his older cousin Gennaro by his wife Alice shared the business of a small restaurant. A modest concern with no carpet and good coffee. Thirty covers. Twenty take-away pizzas every weeknight, fifty on Saturdays.

50:50 cash and card – acceptable.

Elio's share was managing the cooking, the kitchen staff, the waiters, the cleaners, the supplies, the reservations and the bookkeeping. Gennaro's was the cash banking, his personal jewellery, his silver Aston Martin, three mastiffs and a third wife, Adriana. Adriana from Lombardia. The restaurant was Calabrian, an impossible match. So naturally she was never a happy eater at the family table but that's of no consequence to the unfolding of events, as you will see.

The cooks were all aunts. The widow Rosa, Aida, Gabriella the virgin, and Clara. Gabriella was the youngest and therefore stood by the sink. Rosa supervised the food preparation and her station was by the serving hatch. Her eldest daughter Maria was once unhappily married to Gennaro, so Rosa watched him as a kookaburra in a tree does a stump that hides a snake.

Rosa also made several Calabrian signature dishes, her specialty being Spaghetti Alle Vongole. $15 for the entree, $25 the main, all clams designated *vongole veraci*.

A world champion prizefighter once ate lunch there with his many friends and after finishing his spaghetti bolognaise he left the table and walked into the kitchen without so much as a knock on the door.

'Which one of you ladies made the bolognaise sauce?'

He had asked this in a voice made raspy by many blows to his throat. He was holding an empty plate in his hand and looked from aunt to aunt, from eye to eye, a flat-nosed man with big knotted hands and fresh black stitching that threaded above one of his dark eyes. The ladies all paused in their duties a moment. Rosa spoke first.

'What? Who made what?' She was now five years in black.

'This!' he said, thrusting the plate forward. 'Who made this?'

Rosa walked over, looked up at him, down at the empty plate, and sniffed once.

'It was mine.'

The fighter laid the plate down on a bench and kissed her one big smack on her surprised lips.

For eleven years not even her husband Frank had done that to her and her hair still as black as crows' feathers.

'Madre di tutte le divinità,' Aida rolled her eyes and blessed herself. *Aida and men were strangers since the day Vincentio ran away to catch some of the gold at the end of the Thailand flesh rainbows.*

Rosa did not smile until after the boxer had left and the others were back at their work. Only Gabriella the virgin saw it and Rosa alone knew why the girl suddenly giggled at her dishes.

Today, there is a signed picture of this world champion on the restaurant wall. 'Best wishes to Rosa and everyone, Mario'.

~ ~ ~

Now Gennaro's three dogs were kept on his large property at Castle Hill. He had named them after his uncles, Bruno, Avanti and Hercule. He liked the big dogs because they gave him respect and kept everything at the house very private. *You know how these things are.*

You see, Gennaro once had a little trouble with the custom authorities in Marseilles from where he was considering emmigrating to Australia because of a little difficulty he had previously had in Milan. Some of the family who had caused the little difficulty were now living in Maroubra, and one husband and his two sons in particular were untrustworthy. Their parentage was Slovak. The sons were members of an infamous local surfing gang. He worried when cars swept up to his gate late at night and parked with their engines running, nobody getting out.

Meanwhile, Elio was not expected at the restaurant until two o'clock this particular day as his young wife Frattiata was seven months pregnant with their first child and they were both attending an appointment at the doctor's.

They had decided to call the baby Francesca if a girl and Tony if otherwise.

Frattiata loved her Elio so much he was now almost three sizes larger than the boy she had married just four years ago. Her specialty was salmon fettuccine with tarragon cream twice a week and every night early to bed.

So because of this dottore, Elio was not there to take the deliveries.

A great pity.

– for on the same day, the boxer arrived for lunch again with no reservation, accompanied by as many friends from the gym as he had brought with him previously. The group naturally walked through the restaurant to the best tables at the back and took the reserved seats by the pizzeria. By the time Gennaro arrived from the rear courtyard where he had been polishing his Aston Martin they were all smoking and drinking and ready to eat.

Gennaro did not point out that the seats were reserved for a party of five from the bank next door, but what he told his women later was something else of course.

The boxer, sitting deep among his friends, asked if Rosa was cooking today and ordered her bolognaise for all. Eleven plates, same as before. *Rapidamente!*

Naturally, the restaurant owed money to the bank, as do we all, and Elio and Gennaro were planning to add a second storey and verandah with another fifteen tables to the restaurant. A further loan was to be negotiated and the bankers were to have been given the best seats today.

This is also why Rosa was asked to do the restaurant specialty – Prawns Caprice followed by Marinara Filicudi with Taglietelle, Cassata Alla Sicilinia and Lavarzzo coffee – a simple lunch for an Italian, a banquet for a banker. Lastly, a small glass of chilled limoncello, a *digestivo,* and all would be well.

For this meal much preparation was required and that Rosa was not to be interfered with was understood by everyone in the kitchen except Gennaro who suddenly burst in and demanded that she make a bolognaise for eleven without delay.

A grave error of judgment.

Rosa stood very still with her hands full of prawns and flour and said nothing. Gennaro went flap flap flap with his arms and his gold chains jingled and his anger grew shrill.

Rosa said it was impossible. Gennaro replied that not only was it possible but it should be done before the restaurant specialty was prepared for the bankers.

Rosa wiped her hands and gave Gennaro a little anger of her own.

'We have not enough meat sauce – only five or six more plates. Am I a magician? Where do we find more?'

The boxer was standing outside the kitchen door listening to this conversation, having been on his way down the passage to the toilet; the sound of an argument in his native tongue had halted him. In the gymnasium it was either English or Lebanese, both spoken without grace.

'I will fix that problem, it is only a phone call,' said Gennaro with great disdain. 'You get on with the pots and pans and let me run this restaurant. The meat sauce will be here in time.'

The boxer continued on his way. Rosa threw the handful of prawns into a pan of garlic and ginger and asked Clara to find what little bolognaise sauce remained in the cooler. Gennaro went back into the restaurant and rang his cousin Hectore who had a similar business a little way distant. Five Dock after all is Italian more so than Leichhardt.

Hectore said he could spare some meat sauce and would send it within thirty minutes.

Everything for the better, thought Gennaro as he replaced the phone.

A mistake of great magnitude.

Meanwhile –

The doctor told Frattiata that the baby was well positioned and he could see from the sheen on her hair and the light in her eyes that she was happy and well.

Dr Agosta was Genoese and had fathered five daughters.

~ ~ ~

Gennaro's mastiffs required much in the way of feeding, each as much as a young man perhaps, and he had an arrangement for the weekly delivery of their speciality canned food to the restaurant where he could load it into his car to take home. He ordered only the best dog food available, especially for Hercule who had won a blue ribbon at the Palermo Briggadacio re-union a few years back.

All restaurant deliveries were routinely directed to the back entrance and into the courtyard. However, today the courtyard gate was locked because Gennaro had parked his car inside for safety where he could do a little polishing in his spare time.

The delivery man knocked and waited, and nobody came.

A great pity.

The bankers arrived at one o'clock, precisely. All five wore suits and ties and as is the way with timid men who work in offices among women and computers they did not raise a serious complaint when they were seated at an inferior table by the entrance.

A couple of them recognised the prizefighter sitting among his friends by the pizzeria and they made much of being in his company although he was four tables distant and cared not a whistle for the five fat men sitting in the breeze of the open door.

Gennaro visited the bankers' table and with much gusto insisted they take a glass of Chianti with him before ordering. Chianti, like its sister wine Beaujolais, is a rough wine made only for drunkards and women who sit alone at home all day, but Australians don't have this understanding of things. This we all understand and Gennaro perhaps offered it to these important businessmen with loud flourishes if only to engage the attention of a nearby table of countrymen who were visiting Sydney from Griffith to finalise some other kind of business, the type of which is not necessary to mention at this time.

Words in haste lay bodies waste do they not?

Whenever men such as these Griffith men visited the restaurant they usually stayed late and drank much. Gennaro would have liked to take a drink with them if they would allow it, *but on that day the sun will never rise.*

Later, some would say it was like an Italian opera, or a scene from a mobster movie. The restaurant has new furniture now and Gennaro rarely leaves his dogs or the walls of his home in Castle Hill.

Much happened quickly.

Marco was serving Rosa's Prawns Caprice to the bankers when a man entered the restaurant pushing a trolley load of cartons. He proceeded unnoticed almost all the way through the room until he drew level with the boxer's table.

By this time, the fighter and his friends were very boisterous as Gennaro had just informed them yet again that their meal was to be delayed a little longer. A customer waiting for his meal is only happy if he is drinking and the pity is that an empty stomach sends wine to the head a little too quickly. Of all the men at the boxer's table the fighter was the only one who noticed the cases being wheeled past.

'I will fix the problem, it is only a phone call.' '

With an oath of such vulgarity that it silenced not only his own table but every other voice in the restaurant, the fighter rose quickly from his seat and climbed from his chair onto the tabletop. At that moment, Gennaro was once again bowing his oiled head to the Griffith businessmen.

The fighter leapt from table to table on quick and sure feet. Plates of food were scattered noisily to the floor. Bottles of wine fell and shattered. The enraged prizefighter, his eyes grimly set and fixed on his quarry, who had now turned and stood ashen faced and bewildered, rapidly closed the distance between them.

His gymnasium friends followed in a rush of such vigour and momentum that a man of thin blood cried out before fainting into his companion's arms. All the aunts crowded their heads into the serving hatch to witness this unexpected drama.

Behind Gennaro, the big Griffith men stood as one and turned to welcome the advance they mistook as being directed at them. One produced a black handgun from his coat, two others wielded flickering lengths of glittering steel.

Gennaro – now mute with terror – fell backwards into the banker's Prawn Caprice as the fighter launched himself at him, at the *coglione* who would think to serve a Neapolitan bolognaise sauce made of dog food.

Hard Travelling

Grub steps out of his car and walks barefoot across the dusty yard to the back door of the pub. He passes through two large rooms on his way to the front bar, their long counters silent, their lights unlit. A pool table stands heavily gaitered and dust-coated in the centre of one room and a small chalk scoreboard nailed to the wall has the name 'Jacko' scrawled on it.

He buys a schooner from a barmaid with bright red nails and rollers in her hair who's sitting with one buttock perched on a stool. She's listening to the races. The backs of her legs are exposed and have veins as big as worms under the flesh.

He walks out to the front of the building and sits on a long wooden bench set against the wall in the shade, next to an old man wearing a wide-brimmed hat. Beyond them, beyond the car park, long bleached fields rise into the pale forests that crown the distant hills. The hot air weighs heavily. The only birds are caretaker crows. A dozen of them sitting in a spotted gum nearby cursing each other tiredly.

The heat.

Grub is on his way to Adelaide, coming down from Noosa and travelling alone along the inland route, unable to afford a licence check in any state.

Sleeping on an old mattress in the back of his car at nights with only the whining mosquitoes for company. The undersides of his arms are freckled with bites, some have had the itching flesh dug away and they resemble bloody little smallpox craters. Swift settling bushflies cluster in the wounds and feed there.

He snafs them away with a slow wave of his hand.

Grub has got very little cash and the '85 Falcon station wagon that he lives in is making bad noises.

The Insight 6'2' surfboard tied onto the roof has yellowed badly in the two weeks he has been travelling and molten wax has dripped off the deck and pooled onto the car hood. A thousand highway bugs have died there, stuckfast husks with their transit lives windblasted away.

The radio only plays static; the tape deck worked for half a day.

The back window is jammed and immovably half open, half closed. The interior is littered with knots of grimy trodden down clothing and sour towels, blankets, newspapers, fast-food dog boxes and empty plastic coke bottles. A blowfly's litter of maggots knot and unknot amongst the forgotten leavings of an old dinner in the passenger footwell and an offering of feathers, teeth and coloured cloth hangs from the rear-view mirror. The dashtop vinyl has peeled back exposing a thin layer of yellow plastic insulation.

He is many days unwashed and his clothes are stiff with dirt. The stink around the place is the Grub and no other. Grub as he has always been. The soles of his feet are as black as the highway, the calluses on his heels hard as old leather, and his gut boils a stew of bad food and ill sentiments.

Grub drinks half the schooner in two swallows and with his head rested back onto the brick wall of the pub he watches the small marbles of black oil drip ceaselessly from the underside of his Falcon and pool in the shade. The old car settles on one slowly deflating tyre and clicks its hot steel in overheated exhalations. Grub paid $520 for it in Brisbane a month ago.

The dealer was wearing gold rings on all his fingers and a smile yards wide. He gave Grub a full tank of gas to swing the deal and waved him goodbye as he pulled out of the yard.

Grub turns and looks at the old man. The old man is looking at the car. He turns and they look at each other.

'Whatsat on the roof?'

'What's what?'

'Thing on the roof. Deaf are yez?' A toothless mouth denies the old man's intended grin.

You cranky old bastard, thinks Grub. 'Surfboard,' he says.

'What-board?'

'Surf *fucken* board,' says Grub.

The old man stays silent for a moment. He looks down at his hands. Gnarled, big-veined and still. His wrists thick and square, his forearms – sleeved to their elbows – deep with knotted muscle and bound through with cabled sinew. Here and there on his knuckles the faded scars of old settlements and hard-won arguments.

He gets up and goes inside, returning to the bench with another schooner. He sets it down and fingers around in his shirt pocket for the makings.

Grub's beer is nearly finished; the old man's glass is frosted and full. Condensation makes its traceways down the fluted glass and onto the surface of the wooden-topped bench, marked with an interlocking maze of rings.

The heat oppresses, bears down. The crows have gone.

'Me name's Ernie,' he says, 'from Roma.' He pokes a thin smoke into his whiskery mouth and squints over at the kid.

'Smoke?'

Grub takes the makings from Ernie without thanks, slides out a pair of papers and sticks them together.

Then he drops a nub of tobacco onto his palm and tugs a small plastic bag from his jeans pocket with his other hand, he pokes out a little sticky marijuana from this and mixes it in with the tobacco. He rolls the slug into the papers, licks it up and gives one end a final twirl.

Ernie watches from under his hat and pushes over a box of matches. He waits for Grub to light up.

'Whatsat?'

Grub takes a deep pull on the smoke.

'What's what?' He holds the smoke down deep.

'That shit you put in with me tobaccy?'

Grub blows out a thick grey plume, looks at Ernie and smirks.

'Dope.'

The old man takes off his hat and carefully places it on the bench, brim downwards. He cracks a couple of big old knuckles and stands up.

Respect. If not given, must be earnt. Family motto handed down by Grandfather Cec, boundary rider, fettler, drover, tent boxer.

The kid slouches there with his bare feet thrust out, scratching at the dry skin on the back of his hand. He takes another crackling suck of the joint and casts a lazy glance up at the hatless old man who stands there quietly overshadowing him.

Ernie examines the upturned terrain of Grub's face for its weaknesses and sees the close-knit family of them all.

Jaw too weak, nose too bony, cheeks too brittle, eyes too slow.

Teeth too many.

Respect.

Later, after the barmaid had roused herself and given him some paper towels to stop the bleeding, Grub left. Ernie was sitting on the long bench watching him from under his hat, another full schooner by his side and now a russet coloured dog lying at his feet.

A fine red dust filmed the surface of the oil puddle as the ragged blare of the '85 Falcon faded to quiet.

A Bit of Work

Brookvale. 6.30am.

The sudden and soft impact of a currawong chick hitting the ground awoke the rat instantly. The chick's soft yellow beak was impaled into the wet earth and it struggled uselessly with stumped and furred wings. The old rat rustled out of its newspaper nest under the house and stopped at the edge of an overgrown hedge, bristling with hunger. Intent.

Moving as quickly as a snake it rushed up to the bird and seized its rump, piercing the flesh and crushing the young bones. The chick breathed out a soft call of panic to a parent bird who watched yellow-eyed from a high branch by the empty nest.

A black feral cat irritably shook off a dab of water from its front pad as it stepped out of the same hedge and issued a low hiss, arching up and baring broken yellowed teeth in a face flattened with cunning. The rat immediately swallowed a mouthful of feather, fur and flesh then chewed down again, a little electric murmur of bodydeath in his mouth. Warm.

The cat crept closer, mewling like a hungry baby.

Don Hobbs dreamed he was toting heavy hessian sacks into a darkened house where he walked along a narrow hallway, past doors open on either side and into a small room at the rear of the building. Careful here as the floorboards had been removed leaving only the joists. Rotted black posts bristling with nails.

As he lowered his sack onto the ground he noticed again the many others lying humped in the darkness.

A wild-eyed cat crouched among the bodies and howled at him.

Hobbs quickly sat up and swung his heavy legs off the bed, his mouth was dry and foul and his stomach heaved. Turning back to the bed he saw a slim shoulder and arm, short-cropped white hair.

He got off the bed, scooped his clothes and boots up off the floor and left the room, slamming the door behind him. As he washed in the basin he heard the front door close as his overnight companion left the house.

Hobbs lived in a weatherboard ruin of a boarding house on Pittwater Road in Narrabeen. Most of the residents were ex-prisoners or itinerant drifters. The proprietor lived alone in a backyard caravan and raised budgerigars. His boarders paid him ten dollars a night and slept three to a room.

Most days, Hobbs and his mate Raffan sat idle on the front porch until one of them decided to start drinking. They were considering moving up to Brooklyn on the

Hawkesbury River and finding some work on the oyster leases.

After a meagre breakfast of black tea and buttered bread the two men sprawled in an old horsehair lounger on the front porch watching the city-bound traffic stream by. Raffan rolled a thick cigarette and hawked onto the lawn before lighting up.

'Who'd you end up with last night?'

'No idea,' said Hobbs.

They lapsed into contemplative silence.

Raffan stretched out both of his big arms and yawned.

'How you off for dough?'

Hobbs shrugged.

'Not much, what have you got in mind?

'A bit of work.'

'Where?'

'Brookvale.'

Mrs Dickens' Babies

Mrs Agnes Moorehouse was sitting on her porch with her sister Annette sharing a pot of tea they had just brought from the kitchen. Annette's daughter, Mimi, twenty-three months old, had been left sitting in a pool of sunshine by the kitchen door eating a melon slice.

The two sisters had not seen each other for a year and now that the child had been embraced many times there was much to talk about, being women and sisters.

Annette was here for two weeks. Agnes's husband Tim was in India for a month's IT project.

Mimi stared down at the ant who drank from her melon drip, then pressed her fat finger down on both the drip and the ant.

Agnes's best and only dog, a female blue named Mrs Dickens, had lost a litter of two pups to wild dogs some time ago and she hadn't been the same since. She had turned wary of the house and only came close with reluctance. She no longer slept by the porch step. She no longer barked.

Agnes was telling her sister.

'I miss the big girl's company,' she said, 'especially with Tim away. She goes away for days sometimes. I only hope she isn't going wild on me. I worry about what's in the forest up there.'

Mimi got up and followed the trail of ants that wound along the floorboards, down the three concrete steps and then into the back garden. There they disappeared into the grass.

The little girl stood in the sunshine among the flowerbeds and flowering shrubs and looked through the open gate just a little down the pathway. Beyond were the many rises and slopes of the old stallion's paddock, unfenced now, and on the crest of the slope the towering canopies of the top forest, thousands of acres of wilderness.

Mimi walked through the gate. Blonde hair and yellow pyjamas, no slippers – still holding the melon rind. Mimi would sing to herself when she was happy and she always walked in straight lines.

The two sisters only paused when the teapot was cold and Annette went inside for a refill and to check on her daughter.

Mrs Dickens watched the very small person coming straight up the hill towards her. The dog was lying on a bare patch of stony ground between two larger boulders and she could see all the way down to the farm and the creek beyond. Mrs Dickens now spent most of her days here where she had fought the wild dog pack.

The dog sat up when she heard the women calling.

Mimi walked up to Mrs Dickens and stopped for the first time since she had walked through the gate fifteen minutes ago. They looked at each other steadily, eye to eye. Then the child smiled and moved on, straight on, into the trees of the forest.

The big cattle dog stood up, and with one ear tracking the little girl watched Mrs Moorehouse running down to the creek, then someone else rushing out of the back of the house.

Mrs Dickens sniffed the air and growled softly, silently turning to follow the little girl into the forest. She quickly caught up with the yellow pyjamas and by slipping from tree to tree at a distance, managed to keep apace with the little explorer.

Mimi didn't mind the silence and shade of the forest, she only saw the flashes of sunlight around her feet. The bellbird calls. She hummed with her own happiness and walked and walked.

Mrs Moorehouse was on the phone.

'Geoff, Geoff, it's Aggie. Can you get over here as quick as you can, we have a little girl missing. My niece. Hurry, please, she's been gone for half-an-hour already.'

Geoff Southern was the eldest son of the property owners next door and without wasting a moment he ran out of the house and into a large shed where he kicked his Kawasaki motorbike into life. He roared down the gravel drive and gunned the bike overland to the Moorehouse place.

The sisters had searched along the creek first, Annette not daring to think that her little girl had gone there.

Mimi walked her golden way through the forest, not noticing the leech that touched her bare ankle and fell away; the flat red tick that dropped onto her arm from a eucalyptus leaf before sliding off onto the ground – or the nest of bull-ants that boiled out of their mound as she walked by. She didn't notice Mrs Dickens watching her from behind a fallen tree.

How to turn a little person like that? A big working dog can turn a running steer by nipping at its ankles, a wild dog with brute fury, and an unwelcome visitor with just a show of teeth.

What to do here?

Mimi got tired.

She sat down, lay down.

She slept.

Mrs Dickens padded up to the sleeping child and lay down next to her, awake and listening to the whistles from the farm and the whine of a motorbike as it climbed through the fields.

Geoff had already searched the stallions' paddock and was now slowly riding along the edge of the forest whistling for the dog and looking for any sign. The women were frantically searching the creek banks again.

When Mimi woke and saw the dog beside her she immediately set up an almighty uproar. Red-faced and bawling with fright, hunger and cold, and as scared as a two-year old can be. She got up and ran away.

Right into the dog.

Crying even harder the little girl got up again and ran the other way, right into the dog again. Mrs Dickens just stood and watched the child get up for a third time, hoping that this time she would run in the right direction.

At three o'clock, Mrs Moorehouse decided to ring the police. The little girl had to be found before dusk. Geoff had cleared the largest fields and was now in the top forest on foot so he could hear as well as see. Annette was stricken, roaming the creek banks and driveway, desperate to find the child.

Mimi was asleep again, this time up by the stony patch and with the big dog still beside her. Mrs Dickens thumped her tail a couple of times and softly touched the child's face with her muzzle. Mimi got up straight away, taking hold of the dog's ear, and Mrs Dickens woofed quietly as the pair of them started off down the hill, towards the farmhouse and the setting sun.

Senior Constable Terry Hayes was in the kitchen with Mrs Moorehouse and Annette. He was looking at a map of the property spread out on the table and talking into his mobile phone. The two sisters were sitting by the cold stove unable to speak as their thoughts took hold.

Mimi was gone. Three hours now.

Geoff came into the kitchen, dusty and tired, and headed to the fridge for a drink.

'The dog's back,' he said flatly.

Hayes looked up at Geoff who was scarfing down a pint of cold milk.

Mrs Dickens barked once from the front porch.

'Hang on,' said Mrs Moorehouse, 'that's not right.'

They all remained still as Mrs Moorehouse whistled the dog in. She came jogging down the hall and into the kitchen – heading straight for Annette, who sat with her head lowered and pale hands clasped. The big dog pushed her wet nose into Annette's hands and wagged her tail.

Mrs Moorehouse was on her feet and out in the hallway so quickly the crash of her overturned chair nearly drowned out her joyful shout.

'Sis, the baby. She's here.'

Col Joye and the Changing Times

Early every morning
Early every evening too
Early every morning
Early every evening too
I get so lonesome for you
That I don't know what to do

This is what Col Joye was writing when Bob Dylan was wheeling around America singing Woody Guthrie songs.

Col knew his songs were wrong; lyrics are supposed to be reflective of the times you've lived, and here's Bob Dylan taking big chunks out of the domestic record market singing about American death, despair, lynchings and poverty. So Col got into his own ear, told himself to man up. Get into some Aussie *grit*.

It happened that Col Joye had a mate, Ted, lifelong, a friendship never tested, loved him like a brother. So he rang him.

Ted picked up the phone and said g'day straightaway.

'G'day, mate,' said Col, 'goin' alright?'

'Good, Col, you?'

'Not bad, listen, could you do us a favour?'

'Maybe.'

'Your brother still working out of Ultimo?'

'Yeah.'

'Got any room in the car one night does he?'

'For what?'

'Me.'

Col's car was called to the emergency room at St. Vincent's Hospital at 7:45pm on Saturday evening and after parking by the front doors everyone piled outside heading for the noise inside, Col in the rear. *Ready.*

The two officers already inside had collected all the names of the twelve Turks currently in emergency and handed the list to Dave, Ted's brother, Ted being Col's best mate. I've been told that when you write something with a comprehensive bundle of characters it's best to throw in a few *conjoiners* on the way through. Don't want to have the reader flicking back to the character list every couple of pages.

Col eased into the emergency room last and looked for a spot by the wall, found one, slipped a pencil and notebook out of his jacket pocket and took a look around, thinking by the time I get this mess written up into an album and learn how to blow a harmonica, Dylan's got Aussie problems.

Altan was bleeding from a deep laceration to his left palm, part of *Babagidi*'s upper lip had been cut away, *Caetano* was holding his right side, blood seeping through his fingers and *Dagwood*'s left ear had been cleanly cropped. He was holding the piece of bloodied cartilage in his right hand. *Eban* was bleeding from above one ear, his left, the front of *Fass*'s teeshirt was bunched and crimson in his fists and *Gaetan* was examining the depth of a long knife slice in his left arm. All the fingers of *Hadrian*'s left hand were deeply lacerated and his blood dripped steadily to the floor, mixed with that of *Icarus*, whose nose had been brutally crushed. *Jabir* was leaning against the wall, the blood from his shoulder wound seeping down the wall and puddling on the floor around his boots. *Kaarl* sat with his face in his hands, occasionally touching his head where the hair was matted. Blood had coloured his ears. *Lajos* spat another piece of tooth into his hand and swore bitterly.

There had been a wedding. The bride was beautiful, her brothers many. The groom was known to have bad blood, and his brothers *too* many

Everything happened quickly.

An hour later, the police had twelve statements, the emergency room air was clear of Turkic blasphemies and Col followed Dave and Bill down the corridor to the exit. Bill being Dave's offsider. Thinking back on it, Col wondered why they hadn't asked him anything about himself that night. *Col Joye* in the back seat!

Nothing.

The exit door opened inwards six feet before they got to it, another policeman entered, holding what looked like a doctor's bag. Dave, Bill and Col opened up to let him through.

'What have you got in there, Ed?' said Dave. 'Lunch?'

Ed gave a short laugh and stopped. Looked at Col.

'You're that Col Joye bloke, aren't you?'

'Yeah,' says Col, thinking, at last, someone who knows who I am.

'So what are you doing with these two dimwits?'

'Getting a bit of background.'

Ed looked over at Dave and Bill.

'Background?'

Both nodded.

Ed glanced at Col. Looked back at D and B.

'He look hungry to you blokes?'

Both nodded.

Ed opened his bag. Inside, a green garbage bag, open at the top.

Col peered inside

A bloodied head.

'Car accident, body's in the ambo outside.'

Ed closed his bag and walked away.

> *We'll take a vacation*
> *Go away to stay*
> *Where there'll be no work*
> *There'll be nothin' but play*
> *Walk down to the river*
> *To a baby nook*
> *Make a love like they do in a story book.*

Part Two
The Surfer

The Surfer

Women don't look at surfers with the same concentration as we do them. A surfer's glance is better described as a fixed-radius searchlight in that it always goes the same scenic route:

Eyes.
Nose.
Lips.
Neck.
Breasts.
Navel.
Waist.
Thighs.
Knees.
Calves
Toes.

You can add one more if her clothes are on the floor and she's walking towards you, another if she's walking away.

But the lady we think is gazing at us with wistful longing is in fact running her own body check.

Follow us on her journey.

Your eyes

That small trace of white matter seeping from the

corners of your eyes, that redness around the pupil? That's herpetic keratoconjunctivitis: Madras Eye. Not a good look. You'll probably shed a tear as she walks away and that's precisely the treatment your eyes need. How's the irony, eh?

Too bad.

Next.

Your nose

Sinuses are a swamp of embarrassment for the surfer. He knows what has been forced up the sinus passages early in the morning must obey gravity and come back down later in the day but he doesn't know the proper etiquette for mopping up a puddle of nose-water from a girl's navel. Lucky you got that far.

But no further, and too bad.

Knucklehead.

Your lips

The surfer's been in the sun and saltwater all day battling wind and swell and his lips are a little dry, a little cracked – but it's like cool, right? World champion surfer Tom Carroll has been getting away with chapped lips for half his life and still gets profile shots in the magazines.

This matters little with the lady in question because she knows what erythema looks like and it looks like angular cheilitis.

What you have is a fungal farm on your lips and there is no way the lady is going there tonight – so you might as well kiss her goodbye ... like hell.

Too bad.

Next.

Your neck

What could go wrong here? A neck is a neck, all it does is hold up the head and funnel the food.

This lady however knows her way around – and she's looking at your emerging caruncle, your wattle. Twenty years in saltwater have negated all the skin's natural elasticity and now you look like Granma Gettigan down there. Plus there's a small forest of mature hair in the gullies that need attention.

This isn't your day. Know it.

Next.

Your chest

The top-end acres. This is the main attraction. Even if the head is a bit of a pineapple what babe could resist such a fine-tuned torso?

She can because it's not all roses and abs down there, bro. Google how many different terms there are for nipple rash.

Jogger's nipple, surfer's nipple, gardener's (?) nipple, raver's nipple and red nipple. Whatever you want to call it, it's fissure of the nipple, plus there's the possibility that it contains a smear of eczema or a touch of impetigo, a dimpling of psoriasis – whatever, you've got it and she's spotted it.

Dang!

Your navel

It's candida and you read it here first.

Here's you thinking yeast was just for making bread rise. Wrong again, you dill, and the lady is well onto it; yeast is bugs and bugs in the navel is candida and candida is fungus. No good just gazing into there brother, some places need a regular reaming and knowing that Candida was also a hot little Mexican stripper you met in Tijuana in 1973 doesn't excuse you, asamatteroffact there could be more bad news on that front in the future.

Your thighs

Thighs have a neighbourhood problem, and it's the folks upstairs that started it.

We're talking tinea cruris here, eczema marginatum – that's crotch rot: dhobi itch.* You may think that wearing board shorts gives you a fresh air run here but the old travelling jock itch is a little unmistakable in the attention-seeking department – it itches like a bastard.

She sees.

She flees.

Dhobi itch: Back when the English ruled the world and were busy subjugating India they used to have the locals do their laundry – nothing like washing out a gross of old pommie underpants for a living – so the locals put a lot of effort into putting a lot of soap into the wash and not much rinsing it out. The result was some very hard underdaks, hence rash, hence dhobi (laundryman) itch.

Your toes

Most surfers don't worry enough about their toes and as a result have rarely come to terms with the life that teems between them. Trichophyton interdigital, those fellows, they breed like rabbits and don't bury their dead – hence the odour. Footrot is what you've got.

The condition also itches like all the furies and the minute you bend down to give them a scratch that's the game given away. No way tonight will those digits be allowed to touch female flesh

Walk away, lad.

It's over.

Know Your Pleasures

The parents live in a house as big as yours and your neighbours' both sides. The commercial jet flights that puncture every hour of your life are just pretty lights on the horizon here at the end of the drive, the long gravel drive, and somebody has kindly left the gates open, massive wrought iron gothic masterpieces.

You are expected.

The general plan for the evening is to chuck a couple of towels, the wetsuit, a spare teeshirt, the old boardies, the girl and a few bits of fruit into the boot and tie down at least two boards on the roof. Board bags will do for bedrooms. The surfing forecast is for solid perfection all weekend the entire length of the east coast. (just kidding about the girl, she gets a front seat and a footwell)

The girl, we'll call her Wendy, had all but invited herself when she first heard about the trip – and why not, you asked yourself two nights ago at wherever the bar was, and just an hour after you'd met. Alcohol does that to a fellow. Who knows what she looks like tonight but a man is only as good as his word and surely this beautiful girl with long hair, deep brown eyes and treasure upon treasure clad in Chip & Pepper jeans, a

Bench cashmere and wool hoodie is her sister.

But she says *Hi* and plants a kiss on your cheek, then looks over your shoulder at the two-door wreck you arrived in and now you remember the wink from the other night because she does it again.

That's how she got the nod for the trip. It all comes flooding back.

Frank, though, is a little sauced, being Friday night, and that's a Rich Bastard Mogul habit apparently. Frank is Wendy's father, her mother Doreen is in the kitchen. Frank has just the one daughter and is sheltered from all life outside of corporate walls and clubroom bars and you're quickly realising the pure ambience of the evening has yet to settle its radiant aura about his person.

Frank is Big In The City, he drinks Scotch whisky, eats alone every night and watches the NRL every weekend. Frank is not happy with the weekend arrangement concerning his daughter Wendy and this broad-shouldered oaf with his bludger's suntan and unwashed hair. He's thinking that this bloke couldn't hold down a job in a slave-mine, and Doreen never looked at Frank that way either.

Frank measures wealth superficially – as if there is any other way. He's a hair, clothes and shoes man, and this oaf has too much of one and not enough of the other. Frank worries about the big brown bare feet on his Islimi floral shagpile rug.

The oaf – that's you – notices that Wendy is packed and ready for travel. Bag one for clothes, bag two for toiletries and bag three for beachwear, towels and hats. This not inconsiderable mound of matching luggage is stacked by the door and Frank is right up close now with his whisky fumes and eyes all red-mazed up with broken capillaries and here you go again wishing that just one day you and a couple of the corporate Franks of this world might meet in the broken water where all men are equal.

The extraction

It is now seven-thirty in the evening and the schedule is to leave immediately and cover the 950 kilometres before dawn. Point Surf waits for no man. Wendy has already stowed her kit in the car and Frank is beginning to weave around a little just as the stars align in their heavenly traceways and the transcendental mysticism of astral coincidence becomes evident.

His glass is empty, his dinner is ready, the game is about to commence. Frank's trinity of want.

He goes, you leave with Wendy aboard. And five minutes into the trip she puts her hand on your thigh. What to do?

Travelling north

There are times, as it is widely understood, when surfers have a diminished capacity for taking the full and responsible advantage of a lady's polite and well-meaning attempt at seduction. We are not talking about the normal scenario in this instance, the one we are all familiar with where the woman covers herself in hot chocolate and flicks off the bedroom light just as you exit the bathroom in a cloud of masculine lotion and exotic body oils.

So, we're five minutes into the trip north and there's her hand and all her long silver-topped fingernails resting warmly on your thigh; you glance over at her and she smiles the smile of Mona Lisa – then digs a nail in, just so.

Your schedule for the next forty-eight hours

Drive for four hours before stopping at that little pie shop the other side of Kempsey.

Grab a feed.

Drive for another four hours before hitting the Superbank at least half an hour before everyone else wakes up.

Grab a feed at the Coolie sushie bar.

Drive back to Byron via Cabarita, Boggingar, Pottsville and that secret spot just north of Bruns wall.

Grab a feed at the Co-op.

Hit Broken Head, Lennox Head and Boulder.

Grab a feed at the Ballina pie shop.

Her schedule for the next forty-eight hours

Stop the car at the first motel in North Sydney.

Get up in the morning. Late.

Go shopping at Westfield Plaza up by Gosford way. He'll drive.

Spend the rest of the weekend in a Crowne Plaza Terrigal ocean suite.

Buy some chocolate and a bottle or two of body oil on the way in.

He'll understand.

Nothing can prepare a surfer for this test; on the one hand we have nestled beside us a beautiful woman full of the juices of love, and on the other a desperate man six hundred miles away from his love of juice.

There has to be a compromise.

How it all ends

You skipped the North Sydney motel and turned right at Gosford. You slipped down the winding road to Terrigal and booked the top suite at the Crowne Plaza. You sacrificed the hot pies at Kempsy for two room-service pizzas that remain uneaten on the table. There are clothes all over the floor and the beautiful Wendy is an indefinable and fragrant lump in the bed next to you.

And beyond the hiss of the air-conditioning you can hear the faint rumble of waves rounding the point, the Haven. There are waves, there is hope. You stir, she awakes and reaches over, you stir some more.

In summary:

If ever an attractive young woman leans over the bar and looks longingly into your eyes, then breathes a husky wish to accompany you on your next trip to the north, you should think more than twice. You are just another available body in her eyes, an easy means of a weekend's pleasure. Protect yourself: there will never be any more than a temporary satisfaction in conceding to their demands.

Remember the ancient dictum: Once with a woman, twenty times with a wave – know your pleasure(s).

Part Three
The Slaughtermen

The Shute

The uncovered shute rose two storeys high from a large yard in the front of the building, built narrow enough for just one beast to fit and steep enough to keep the line of them unbalanced; built of sheet steel, it solidly defied all attempts to kick the sides down and the day-long procession up this final walkway and towards the gun chamber provided a thunderous percussion to the everyday chorus of misery.

The topmost beast was hot-prodded onto a level platform at the head of the shute then enclosed by a steel trap lowered by the slaughterman. Les Heath worked there alone for each of his ten-hour shifts, and in his fastidious way he executed up to two hundred and fifty beasts each day before making his way back to the small cottage he leased behind the southern corner of Broken Head.

Les was a small man cruelly fashioned with a kyphosis hump and a lifelong aversion to direct sunlight; men who had worked with him for over thirty years had never seen him without his hat. He was a silent man with deep religious convictions and an abiding patience for the three lads perched behind him on the outer wall eating their lunch, chattermouth kids leaning over to watch him place the muzzle of the bolt gun against the head of the trapped beast.

Placid as the gun was settled on their foreheads, and at times their eyes rolled upwards to their executioner in dumb trust the instant his bolt smashed through their skull.

Jimmy and John, the Islander brothers, and Pete, no longer the new boy; sitting up there like magpies on a telegraph pole waiting for a rabbit to be run over.

There were times when one of Les's poll knockers failed to kill a hard-headed beast, and when he released the trap that dropped the semi-conscious animal onto the blood-floor it would stagger upright and scatter all the black-aproned butchers to the walls until one of them managed to seize the sledgehammer and deliver a blow to its head hard enough to knock it back down. Then he would immediately bend over the animal, draw its head back and slice open its throat, standing over it in a hot slick of blood, hammer ready, until death was certain.

The three lads on their feet now and lunches forgotten, crowding Les out of his stall for a better look, whistling and catcalling advice to the slaughtermen below, hoping for a bloody uprising and final charge from the catastrophically maimed beast, wanting, without knowing, a rich spill of men's blood here to balance the bloodletting. Watching the six butchers blunder about on the wet floor in panic and in particular the one known to have the other men's wives on his playlist.

And his troubled eyes were for his colleagues, not the staggering beast as it bumped and bled and finally submitted to the crushing blow of a twenty-pound sledgehammer.

He heard the mocking catcalls from the shute-top that betrayed the whole town's knowledge, and in the midst of the improvised slaughter of the undead beast his upswept glance took all of us in, and his ledgers were posted as being owed, and in the years to come many of these dues were collected.

2am and the backdoor bangs open as the drunk careens into his darkened kitchen pulling up hard against the table and in the moment of quiet before he aims his truculent body towards the hallway and bedroom he hears a scurry of movement and the soft scrawl of a window being raised.

He is handy with a knife, but his rush up the blackened hallway is hindered by his drunkenness and when finally he stands in the doorway of the bedroom she is lying quiet there and cool air pours through a window rarely open so wide.

'Three weeks later, Les fails to knock a hardhead over and the cow gets upright on the blood-floor and needs another killing. All the butchers duck away to the walls until it's over and I'm watching Mick the Pom to see where he's looking. Someone else grabs the hammer for a change and if Mick backs into me he's going to wear my knife in his kidney at last.

He's wary, looking everywhere but at me, and now he's looking at the bloody kids up there with their racket and piss-taking, trust those little arseholes to know shark bait when they see it.'

The Cooking Room

A dark passageway, all the walls wet and over there a young man racking up a firehose. He watches you pass by. The smell in here is overpowering, warm and fecund, and all around is the hiss and clank of superheated boilers as they cook up the slaughter floor waste. Two massive iron cylinders sitting a metre off the floor on concrete footings.

A mezzanine where two men take up the trolly-loads of waste, tip it onto the floor in a jellied mess of skulls, offal, flesh, hooves and bones – thigh high. They shovel these remains into open boiler hatchways that belch great gusts of steam.

The boilers have their internal thrasher arms engaged, great swinging iron arms that pulverise the waste as it boils and breaks down into a bubbling red festering mud.

Curly runs the cooking room. A cocksure fellow with clean hands and twenty years put away. He takes you over to the gauges and the chains that govern the temperatures and pressures. He walks you around to the boiler face and shows you how to open the discharge hatch and take a sample of the cook.

The other men stand around the walls watching, smoking, grinning. Some of them you remember from the Great Northern that night everybody was beaten. Five minutes of pure mayhem, playtime for the local men.

The latch on the discharge hatch had to be engaged, the hatch opened only millimetres, a small drool of cooked matter caught on a hessian rag held out on a shovel, the hatch refastened and the drool tested by folding the hessian over and seeing if it sticks to both sides.

Take down the pressure, stop the flailing arms, open the discharge hatch wide and watch the superhot larva pour into the enclosed steel tray at its mouth. Close the hatch, engage the hydraulic lift, attach its chains and hooks to an empty centrifuge container and lift it over to the floor close by the tray, take a shovel, slide up the front side of the tray and load the centrifuge container. It bubbles like bolognaise. Spits. Burns.

When the container is full, lift it over and settle it into the centrifuge mechanism then look around for a cap that might fit. Some are less than round. Find one, use the hydraulic lift to settle it on the container, lock it down, drop the centifuge lid and lock that down then flick the mechanism on.

Listen to the centrifuge grumble up its revolutions to a great groaning roar, guard against the lid coming off its fasteners as the speed increases.

Apply the brake when necessary, that's the wooden post by the side of the centrifuge. You have to stand on it and apply leverage, and keep bent over in case the lid flips up. The container is whipped around inside the centrifuge at an ungoverned speed, metal screeches against metal. Let the machine slow, lift the centrifuge lid, unlock and lift off the container cap, then lift out the container and upend the dried contents into the milling pit.

That's it, that's what you have to do. Tomorrow. The process removes tallow from the waste. The dried matter is then milled, bagged and piled in a corner of the shed. Doug does that, he's had the job for fifteen years.

There is a doorway off to the side of the cooking room that leads to a narrow walkway which is cooled by the north-easter; this is where Curly and his two offsiders stand as you take to the job. The room itself is almost unbearably hot and the hiss and roar of steam and machinery drowns out all other sound. We work bare-chested with only hessian rags to protect our hands. Small cuts and abrasions gather up the filth and poison the blood but there is no first aid box, no workers' compensation, no sick leave.

We work twelve-hour round-the-clock shifts and after three months there is an unqualified acceptance. There is room on the breezeway wall for the Sydney boy and a place in town on Saturday night when the Brisbane surfers come roaming down from their city.

Thinking they can't be beaten.

The Loading Gang

Franco slid them out of the rooms ten at a time, all hanging from a greased running rail that led from the coldroom to the railway dock where the freezer car waited. Half-sides of beef hung by their Achilles tendons, all of them chilled solid and quality stamped, ready for the Brisbane meat markets.

Three hundred pounds in weight each. One thousand half-carcasses to the truck, three trucks to the line. Three hours for the load to be done. A lifting game of heavy weights and balance and dogged perseverance.

Two tally clerks stand around in their fresh whites, clipboarded up, and knowledgeable enough to dodge out of the way of a swinging side of beef deliberately mishandled. Poxy little bastards with their clean fingers and polished shoes, and not a drinker among them.

Myth has it that Archie, head ganger twenty years ago, knocked over one of these office maggots with an open side of beef and the exposed rib bones sliced away half his face.

Two men came out of the bar door and onto the street and took him by his arms, him just passing by the hotel on his way home from the shed, a long walk to the Pass, and they hoisted him over the hotel step and through the public bar doors and inside the room where a more men from the killing shed were drinking after their pre-dawn shifts and who all stopped to see what attraction this particular commotion might produce.

They pushed him up against the bar and demanded that he stay with them, and drink with them until they had all had drunk enough, and then join them for a counter lunch of peas beef gravy and potatoes, and then drink on into the afternoon until weariness won over from thirst, and from time to time they asked him where he had come from, and where he hoped to go to, and why he was here.

This surfing nonsense.

They clapped him on his bloodied shoulders and rubbed his long salty hair, they gathered around him all day and swept him up and included him as one of them, this Sydney boy, this gangman.

Jimmy's Red Merc

Jimmy Keevers – you have to picture him. A skinny goofy-foot with a happy light in his eyes as we sit on the Brunswick south wall looking at the breaking sweep of a set of waves. He went, I stayed. Jimmy had five boards under his house, I had one on top of his car and the wall was eating them up that day.

They took me into Jimmy's pig-pen the day Walkers was hiring, asked me to sit and wait while they got things sorted in the office. Ten minutes later, one of them poked his head around the door to see if Jimmy had scared me away with his slow-motion pig killing technique. Now there was a bond made in heaven; we got on so well I had lunch with him and his brother later on, up at the top of the shute, watching Les ping cows with his bolt gun. Johnny surfs Wategos every morning these days I'm told, and loves to have everybody share his waves, just like the old days.

Believe it?

Jimmy drove a battered, red Merc battleship through Byron town one day with ten boards stacked onto the roof and ten heads hanging out of the windows all yelling at us how good it was going to be wherever they were going. That car rained red rust on tarmac.

Jimmy's a little rusty now; he must be 70 plus, like me. He has a younger brother in town, Sput, the spaceship boy. He runs a business on the strip and here we are today leaning over the counter and he asks, when did you last see Jim?

'63.'

Jim's in Brisbane, under care after a big black stroke hit him when he was 33.

Here's to ye, old friend. I hope someone tells you I remember.

Surf's been up, they say.

Part Four
Outward Bound

The School

The Outward Bound School was founded by Kurt 'The Rod' Hahn, a German-born Jew who respected the views of youth yet didn't mind handing out punishments to those he thought unworthy of the standards he set them.

The Australian OB school was opened in 1956 at Fisherman's Bend, just around the corner and up a long reach from Milson's Passage which is itself is a just a couple of miles upriver from Brooklyn, a half hour north out of Sydney by train.

Brooklyn, named after the Yank engineers who built the Hawksbury River bridge some say. A ragged little town built around oyster leases and on top of mangrove mud. Mosquitoes and shitpans brimful of blind maggots – rivermen and their secrets. The bedlam at Peat Island, a madhouse without walls.

We would motor by the island, see them standing up to their knees in the mud just yards away and howling at us, men and women – unclothed. So permanently wretched. The few who survived the river crossing scattered into the high sandstone gorges and died in caves with fire-blackened roofs where the Darugs once sheltered. Bones upon bones.

The Hawksbury school has a Wikipedia entry which lacks preciseness in that there is no mention of the boys who drowned on an expedition on the Hume Weir in the winter of 1963.

One boy laid out on the ground while we sheltered near a fire. We warmed ourselves and looked at his still form, cold rain gathering on his face and clothes, beyond shelter.

This was after the Duke met me. That summer morning at Circular Quay. Sunday.

My father sent me to the school for a month's course, sent me to learn – to learn obedience, to learn respect, and to straighten the fuck up. I was eighteen. Hair too long, friends too wild, habits too bad. Drunk and disorderly. Disaster.

In 1963, the Queen and Prince Philip came to Sydney and arrangements had been made for him to hand over an ex RAN motor boat to the school on a Sunday morning, the morning after the course ended. The morning after a major celebration at the Watsons Bay Hotel where old habits were temporarily resumed and old friends were gathered.

We stood in two lines, all the Outward Bound old boys and their instructors. Philip came down the Brittania's steps and began his informal inspection, looking left and looking right. Everyone in suits and ties, standing at attention, respectful. Smiling.

Everyone but two.

That lad there … ! The one without a tie or a coat, the one with his hair over his collar, him!

He walked over quickly and looked down and said hullo, looked hard into the lad's eyes and asked a few questions – What do you do? Where are you from? What do you want to be? – and always this half-smile on his face. Here's a man worth knowing.

– and a hundred yards away, behind the wooden barricades where hundreds of people were gathered, my mother is shouting – 'My son … ! He's talking to *MY SON*!!'

He wished me luck and walked on.

Ed Reid was standing with the other instructors at the end of the lines, he too had no tie. No coat.

Years later, we toasted the Queen's husband, sitting in the dark lounge of an east Sydney hotel, Ed and me, both of us older and even more unsettled by life and how it had evolved since that day.

Like marriage is this life – it surely is for better or for worse.

The Initiation

March. 1961. Fisherman's Point, the Hawkesbury River.

Forty-one degrees and a northwesterly looks like any other wind on the water up here, where the beaches are made of mud and mosquitoes know no sunset.

Scoresby, ferry-bound with about forty others, gazes with the stupefaction of the kidnapped at his home for the next forty nights.

Blackmud beach, winding goat tracks wandering up to some unpainted timber shacks under the meagre shade of skinny-limbed eucalypts all monstered by the droning shrill of the world's best cicada population.

Outward Bound Camp.

A knot of instructors wanders away from the jetty as the ferry disgorges the latest intake, some stopping a little way off to observe the new boys, others disappearing into the darker grottoes of the surrounding forest.

Most are barefoot, bare-chested. Skinny looking men. Bearded. Glacially unemotive. Nobody waves.

Later we find out that these men have climbed every mountain and walked every glacier, they have crossed every polar continent and mapped all manner of wilderness, swamp and ruin upon the earth.

Now they are here, as are we, at the behest of either an optimistic employer or a disappointed parent. Payback.

Chief Instructor Ed Reid had someone bust his nose more than once and this, together with a pair of tattooed forearms, unblinking eyes and quiet voice, was enough to have the newcomers listen in complete silence.

'You will dump your bags into your huts,' he intoned, 'now. You will then immediately regroup in front of the mess-hall in single file. You will enter said hall and sit at the tables, four a side. And you will not talk to anyone for the duration of your meal. If you want something, you will wait until somebody else notices and offers it to you.'

Instructor Ed Reid, veteran of two twelve-month sojourns to the Antarctic, wireless operator and haircutter for Bill Tillman on his Big Ben expedition. Scoresby, small youth of the present, wishing that this were some kind of dream.

Try sitting at a table with seven others and wanting the salt, or the pepper, or the bread or butter, or impossibly, the jam. Seven other strangers who have already, by some kind of transcendental mental connection, decided to deny you any and all of the above items.

Strangers like David from Wahroonga, church-educated and a foreigner to sport, drinking and the normal bastardry of acceptable Bondi behaviour.

Like Kevin from his grazier family's property up Moree way, Joey's boy, rugby freak, school handball champion for the past four years. Prefect, class captain. Or Oseve from Papua. Pidgin English, feet like leather-tonged plates, teeth like whitened ivory and a laugh like some kind of hysterical angel.

Like Antony, a cold lonesome bastard from somewhere deep in the city, who listened to no overture, who needed no friend, yet who wept after two days of exposure to the rain and cold on the way back from Staples Lookout.

Or like the boys who died later that year in the cold waters of the Hume Weir when the weather turned to icy treachery and a squall flipped their canoes. Miles from shore. One instructor found dead high up in an ancient water-bound tree. Stiffened by the freezing wind.

A young uncovered body over there, laid out in the rain. Parents unknowing.

Everyone got broken that day

Two years later Scoresby and Reid met in a hotel in Chippendale and sat around for a while not saying much. Eyes hardly meeting, mostly just drinking. Cigarettes and rum, done damage done. He brought his wife along that last time, the shy English girl with dark eyes.

Both gone now, untraceable, lost but to memory.

Ed died two days ago in Tugun Qld. (16 Jan 2011) – seaman, artist, navigator, sailor, Outward Bound instructor, Antarctic veteran, teacher. He was a friend to all who knew him.

The Last Heroes

Back in 1995, Tim Madge wrote a book about a bloke called Bill Tilman called *The Last Hero*. The 278 pages probably sold about a hundred copies to school libraries that didn't mind turning out boys who would rather climb hills than corporate ladders.

Tilman was a lonesome servant of the latitudes. He drove men and boats, strings of climbers and hard-bitten wanderers to the airy edges of the void of their manly aspirations.

Bill Tilman was a knuckled-down kind of man with a gouged out architrave of a forehead lined like a homecoming groundswell, and he sucked a pipe that would have satisfied a room full of potheads. He washed as insincerely as an Englishman does in the tropics.

Tilman explored high mountains, distant reaches and wild oceans.

Years ago, he came through Sydney on a discovery path to Heard Island and as a seventeen-year-old boy I sat on the floor of a survival bush school (Outward Bound) in the Hawkesbury River at the feet of the lucky ones who were to accompany him to the

Antarctic; wrenched through and through with the desire to be with them and travel to that place. I was overlooked as too young, but I still revel in the memory that I was *considered*.

I don't know anyone who knows Ed Reid: his busted nose and hard-handed grasp, his ancient understanding of antagonism and its futile warranting, his clean thinking and patient listening to the bullshit that assailed him from all of the kids at Outward Bound.

Kids from Waverley and Joeys, and kids from Walgett and Bourke and Papua.

Ed sailed with Tilman and Tilman climbed with Shipton. Hillary used their maps in his early exploratory climbs around Everest.

Just names now, so pass them by, reader.

Ed and I sat one night in the common room of the Outward Bound's Hawkesbury school back in about 1960, and as the fire died away he chuntered on about the Antarctic and how a hundred yard right looked breaking down the side of a sunken moraine in minus 15 degrees temperature.

He remembered the wind as an evil thing.

One side of the room was bookshelved to the ceiling and stacked with volumes that denied many seventeen-year-olds their just sleep.

Hillary, Conrad, MacLean, Fleming, Smythe, Younghusband, Buhl, Villiers, Shackleton, Worsley.

There was a picture in one of the books of a young George Mallory, lost on Everest in 1924, a climber, it was said, who could 'flow' up vertical rock, here seen striding shamelessly naked while leading a string of animals to the base camp on an earlier trip to Everest, and in the background a crenellated wall of mile-high ice-covered cliffs, all unclimbed.

Years later I learnt Mallory was a member of the Bloomsbury Group, he and Ed would have got on fine.

RIP Ed Reid.

Part Five
Places

Lismore

Lismore tattoo shops have softer seats and better coffee than those down on the strip – although the Byron parlours have a better looking female customer base – backpackers and the like. Plenty of long brown legs.

Lismore looks after its own. Dave for instance, he's in the chair today after having had all his hair cut off back at the farm by his brother, Mick.

I asked Dave why he was having fifteen skulls and a Harley Davidson 1997 Shovelhead inked onto his newly shaved head.

'Who's going to see it when your hair grows back?'

'Don't be stupid,' he says, 'I'll have somethin' to look forward to when I go bald.'

Dave's a bit of a hardnut, like Janice.

Janice does checkout duty at Coles in Lismore Square, been there for fifteen years.

Janice is a big unit, short, fat and wide. She also has eyes that would rival Elizabeth Taylor's.

She, Janice, applies sparkle to her eyebrows the same way a woman puts on expensive perfume when you have to be close to catch the fragrance. The closer you get to Janice the less you see of anything other than her eyes.

$235.00.

Janice looks at me.

'You have Fly-Buys?'

'Only if they get me a ticket to Hong Kong tomorrow.'

She laughs, soft and husky.

'Not likely.'

I swipe the card, wait for the docket to spill out and take it from her.

'You know something?'

'What?'

'If this counter wasn't between us I reckon we could score a hug here.'

'Don't let that stop you,' she says.

Janice walked out of her checkout, came right up close and wrapped her arms around me. Her head was about as high as my chin.

... and her perfume wasn't too bad either.

Lismore, my kind of town.

Avalon

I was reminded of Avalon the other day by Dave. *Early '90 to 2005 – prime time.*

We were talking about Roy when Realsurf had a man on Avalon station, the time Roy was muscle on stone. He only talked to surfers he didn't know when it was time for them to go in.

But he did wave his arms around a lot on his backhand bottom turn.

This is what I told Dave:

Back in the day when I was taking pics of Avalon for Realsurf – especially the good days at south Av when the left broke into the pool – Roy would spot me from the water and give me a little wave. I thought it unusual. The Avalon Mafia wasn't happy with me at the time and Roy was up there in a hierarchical sense. Then, later the same morning, I'm having a cup of tea on the verandah and there's a knock on the front door. It's open. There's Roy. Smiling.

'Get any of me?'

Then we talked about *Krausey*. This bloke came out of the volatile bottle, so I helped him fizz. It helped that old Krausy was bigger than me because in my book if things get so difficult somebody has to punch someone it has to be the little bloke who punches first, otherwise it looks bad.

This is how that went:

Krausey had a front row North Av car park spot one new year morning, alone in the car. I'm just over by the fence with a few mates and they all know how things are between me and the big K so I say to them, watch this.

I walk over to Krausey's passenger-side window, it's open, I stick my face in and when he turns around to see who it is, I say, happy new year, then offer him my hand. He took it.

Peace on earth, and in Avalon.

Brookvale Revisited

1975

The Brookvale Mafia.

Pick up the mail on the way to work was the order of the day. Park in one of the slots behind the arcade, walk through and cross Pittwater Road to the Brookvale post office. Simple enough, except on this day there were two men silhouetted at the mouth of the arcade, the Pittwater Road end, both leaning against the grimy, curtained windows of the Chinese chop shop that fronted the street.

Big men, unwashed, unshaven, sullen. Watching as I approached. One was clutching a dirty rag, the other had his hands in his pockets.

Eddie Chan was expected to be early today, being Monday, even though his restaurant wasn't scheduled to open until eleven. And he knew they would be waiting for him, his window-washers, because his glass would be broken tonight if his insurance wasn't paid today.

Timing is everything.

The Head Shop.

Someone asked me to buy them a hookah; they planned to fill the bubbler with Pernod on party night to see if the smoke came out sweeter.

The Head Shop had a narrow frontage on Pittwater Road and came with an emaciated youth who slouched behind the counter. Everything inside was dusty, the shop dimly lit. His display was of cheap, Chinese-made doper's bric-a-brac. Tobacco tins, bongs, trimming scissors, seed containers, over-sized cigarette papers, carved wooden hash pipes and the world's oldest collection of High Times magazine.

'Before you go,' he said, 'I've got a photo of a house to rent if you're interested.'

I waited for him to pull out his wallet and extract a creased photo of the back of an unpainted wooden hovel, a set of rickety stairs leading to an upper level, an unkempt lawn, a couple of misshapen trees and two skinny marijuana plants in the foreground.

I handed it back.

'Not today.'

Nothing grows well in Brookvale.

On the Hill

You know that song of Nick Cave's, Into My Arms – the one with a melancholy hook, well that wouldn't have been out of place the other day on the hill. Sitting up there with TonyF and Ross the Kiwi.

Cyclone Oswald had ripped through the strip of forest that separated this place from the nut farm down the valley, thirty trees on the ground, swiped. Ross has the heavy mulcher, TonyF the chainsaw – together they chop the fallen stuff out and spit the mulch back.

Everyone has lunch and we sit on the hill looking west at midday, at the shadows and rain storms moving about the Nightcaps. A wilderness of forest and ranges peopled by men and women who had fled the cities.

Wild dogs, long-legged and alert, with the eyes of a cat and the ears of a fox. They stop and look at the car as we drive past, curious, and sniffing for warm blood in all that noise. Women who don't bother washing their children, ancients bound to their rooms by the overpowering growth of forest and vine about the rotted timber they sleep under. Mould in their rooms as high as moss on a damp rock. They cough all night, wet to the lungs.

Pretty boy that dog, my wife said as we rattled past on the rutted gravel.

Two short rifle snaps at dawn this morning as a neighbour pulled on some warm pups leaving their den.

Just over the fence. Sometimes he waits in the forest for hours.

Pretty boys.

'You realise,' says Ross, 'that we are without any real consequence in the run of things in this country. We matter not a diddle.'

Ross has seven children and therefore seven times the patience of a man with one, and he leans back onto the warm grass, passes on the shared smoke, and measures his words for reasonableness.

The 12.40 Jetstar from Ballina to Sydney slips past in the eastern sky.

'Can't figure those city puppies,' he finally says, 'always afraid of the boss, always shitting themselves about their job. Leaving little to chance.'

He looked at TonyF, who was nearly asleep.

'What do you say, bro?'

'Don't gamble, mate,' TonyF said. 'Chance is just hope's fleeting shadow.'

The Gates of Mount Jerusalem

Sometimes a man takes a wrong turn in life. He heads off another way and becomes lost.

Road signs will help you do that.

Wayne Berrigan had a delivery the other day – a package to be delivered to Kunghur. This place is a little way over from Uki, which itself is south-west of Mur'bah. That's half an hour off the Pacific Highway to Queensland. Just past Mullum'.

Going in was easy. Go past the Mooba' hotel, travel over the Burringbars, turn left before Dunbible, then left to Stokers Siding, Smiths Creek, Uki and then onto the road to Kyogle. Then find the right property and the job's done.

Wayne was pretty happy with that, being the first time he's gone that way – through the Border Ranges, around Warning and under the Rim.

Even in sunshine there is a gloom there with the massive overshadowing.

Coming back, Wayne stopped by the war memorial in the middle of Uki looking for a name which wasn't there and that's when he took the wrong way out of town.

Yet a little further along there was a road sign that said *Mullumbimby,* so this must have been the way in. Must have been.

So Berrigan carried on, and cranked up the volume.

How they tell it.

'What do you reckon of a bloke,' this fellow at the bar of the Mooball Hotel says, 'who tries to convince himself that he *saw* that forty-year-old tin shed tied onto an old table-top truck stuck in the middle of a paddick, an old blue table-top, saw it on the way in ...!?'

Nobody reckoned. That was the old Godfrey place, deserted now and full of Mrs Godfrey's cats gone wild.

'Or the two-storey mound of vine by the side of the road that had an old timber toll house in its middle – with a bloody light on ...! Or the three causeways two foot under running water. Normally you would remember at least one of those, particularly the one with all the ducks, but not Berrigan. Berrigan carried on going his way because he had convinced himself that he'd seen all this stuff coming in and had forgotten it all going out.

Forgotten Godfrey's shed, the truck, the old toll house, the flooded causeways – and the bloody ducks. But if the sign said Mullum then Mullum was at the end of that particular road. Not a complicated man Berrigan. Just a bit dim.'

Then the road went to gravel, and started to climb. An empty dumpster cannonaded past him at the bottom of a narrow passage and Berrigan glimpsed the crazy smile of the driver as he crashed past. Then mile after mile of narrow gravel winding through gorges and heavy forest. No homes up here, no more traffic.

First gear now and the road is heavily rutted and very steep – too narrow to turn around. Berrigan could now only go higher and deeper.

Somewhere up there must be an end to it.

The historic nightcap walking track to Mullumbimby starts at the entrance to Mount Jerusalem Park, at the very gates. At least there's enough space to turn around up there.

Sydney

A boy of about ten has stopped mid-stride in the middle of the Corso's pedestrian traffic; they have to step around him as he holds an iPhone up to his face with both hands, his thumbs working.

Frozen. Still life. But for the thumbs.

Brazilians, Chinese, Koreans, English … women with prams, men with their surfboards, boys on skateboards, chattering schoolgirls, an unsteady drunk. They don't interest the boy as they weave around him.

He's a statue.

Then he scores.

Punches his small fist into the air and turns to a woman sitting on a bench about twenty feet away. She's looking elsewhere so he scarpers over, shows his mum the display then lifts another fist into the air.

The restaurant

They had responsibly-farmed, skin-on, pan-fried barramundi with paperdelle pasta and, among other tasties, a tablespoon of passion fruit dabbed here and there. The waitress, Rosalie, told us she was from

Colombia and she learnt tonight that when a Chinese customer tapped the table with one finger he was saying thank you, that will be all.

'Muchas gracias, senor,' she said, 'now I have learn something.'

There were three men in the open-fronted kitchen: Archan Boumedianne, Rasly Shaktyr and Fernandez from Sri Lanka. They weren't busy with only four tables occupied so at the end of the meal and after paying Rosalie I walked over to the counter that separated the kitchen from the floor, caught Archan's attention and asked him if he had a passion fruit handy.

He sent Rasly to the pantry to find one and I waved Fernandez over. He was only slicing tomatoes.

When Rasly returned I asked if they knew why such an ugly little thing was called a passion fruit.

Archan, the head chef, waited for his two underlings to commit themselves before joining them in shaking his head. Negative all around on that.

There were two knives on the counter as well as the fruit, a serrated bread knife and a large pointed cutting knife.

'May I?'

Archan nodded.

I picked up the fruit and using the tip of the cutting knife wounded its wrinkled parchment-like skin, making a thumb-sized hole.

I put the knife down, lifted the passion fruit to my mouth and sucked it dry.

A Small Town Welcome

Awelcome was hard earned here, and almost always conditional. Byron Bay usually defended itself against any newcomer with either blank-faced rebuffal or a beating.

The town had no shortage of strong-armed men with both the butter factory and the slaughterhouse in full production, and any young visitor from the cities to the north and south faced a frightening series of gauntlets before being given any measure of acceptance.

You've been drinking in the public bar of the Great Northern every night since you arrived on the train from Sydney, up for a few months of long waves and winter warmth.

Everybody in the bar knows your business but you are yet to receive a friendly word from any of them. Though you try.

Three men are drinking at a table by the door, there is one spare seat and you ask if it's taken. And of course it is, even though the fourth man who was sitting in it left an hour ago to start his twelve-hour shift at Norco.

An old man is lounging in a corner of the bar listening to a Brisbane League game, he has his smokes, his form guide, a schooner and a double tot of OP rum all set out on the bar in front of him – like a widower's picnic – and when you ask him what the score is, not that you really want to know, he talks over your shoulder to the three blokes sitting at the table by the door. He asks them howcome the railway is giving free tickets to Byron for idiots from Sydney.

The café is quiet at 7.15pm and all the booths are empty. They shut at about eight, so half an hour should be plenty of time to buy a feed of sausages and eggs. But the waitress doesn't appear right away. She's in the kitchen talking to someone, you can hear her laughing, and after ten minutes she comes back through the swing doors.

She walks around the booths one by one and picks up all the menus from the tables, including yours; she stacks them by the cash register. Then she upends all the stools on top of the counter and turns off the outside light. It's 7.30pm.

The kitchen light goes out and a back door closes.

You wait.

Nothing moves on the street outside.

The waitress glances at you as she wipes down the counter and you hear a car pull up outside with a little tyre squeal. A car horn sounds once. Then all is quiet again. You get up from the booth and walk to the door.

Outside, the boyfriend is leaning up against his car. He wears his shirtsleeves rolled high to show his heavy arms and as you walk outside he pulls himself upright and takes a step in your direction.

He is wearing narrow black jeans and a clean white shirt, he's barefoot, unsmiling, and looks heavily tanned, and there is no seeing into his eyes tonight.

He hits you on the side of the head and the café's glass window bends like plastic as you fall against it, only to rebound into the second blow, this time to the stomach. Down now.

The waitress leaves the café and locks up the front doors, then walks around you and climbs into the car. You notice that she has nice legs, and he is still standing there undecided, so you bleed a little onto the footpath in submission, waiting for him to go away.

A youth in a Freshwater Surf Club teeshirt has taken a small calibre rifle from his car and is walking towards the beach. He's with about three or four others and they have all been camping at the Pass for a couple of days enjoying the swell; taking aggressive ownership of the lines that bend around the Cape and peel away through Wategos and then around the Pass. They are all excellent surfers, strong and quick, and one of them has earned some notoriety from a well-publicised trip to Hawaii the previous year. This is their last day at the Bay before continuing on up the coast to the Queensland points.

The fellow with the rifle squats down behind the fishing boats that have been drawn up to the high-water mark and takes a bead on a silver gull. He has no shortage of targets today as birds are feeding in the tide ponds in their hundreds.

Silver gulls, terns, Pacific gulls, pelicans and black-tails. A couple of oystercatchers are sleeping beside a mound of stinking kelp and wave after wave draws away down the cove in the windless air. This is not a day for killing gulls.

A tossed stone scatters the birds to the air at the same time as the youth pulls the trigger, and he turns to see who has betrayed his intent. Another young man is standing up on the grassy knoll that overlooks the boat ramp, from where he shies another and heavier stone, this time at the shooter, and with greater accuracy.

There follows a vociferous engagement between the two that ends when the fellow with the rifle retreats to his car. His three friends have now joined him, and half a dozen local youths, including a few Islanders, have wandered down from the Pass lookout to watch the confrontation. Standing with them is a young giant of a man.

The Freshwater car spits gravel all the way up to Lighthouse Road leaving the stone thrower, a Sydney boy, alone with the group of local surfers.

One or two smile at him, and the big fellow comes over close, he's barefoot, unsmiling and heavily coloured.

There is a benign recognition in his eyes and he extends his oversized hand.

Part Six
People

Noah

Noah sits in a wheelchair on the verandah of his home in the hills most days.

He's about eight and lights up a smile every time he sees you looking at him. Then he gets goofy because both his front teeth are gone and he looks away, back to the trees.

Trees like the ocean's swells. As distant, as silent. Moving.

Noah is profoundly deaf, born with a neurological condition that also blessed him with total body numbness. He has walked on broken glass and tracked smears of blood through the house. But now he has learned to sit and watch the trees bend this way and that under the strength of the summer north-easterlies.

He often waves back.

Lindsay

There's not much to show of Lindsay; he's about seven stone in weight and his arms and legs are like double-jointed tomato stakes under his clothes.

Today, he's put together in a new, twill-grid check royal blue shirt, wide leather belt and sharply pressed dark blue duds. New loafers, knitted socks. Lindsay is hard of hearing in both ears but only bends his head to listen from his right side. Which means I have to lean across him and SPEAK VERY LOUDLY.

We are in the big room at Ballina RSL at about dinner time. Men and women of massive proportions pass by our table, heading for the food lines. Lindsay watches a lumbering family pass by, turns to me and slowly raises an eyebrow.

'I used to be a plumber.'

'YOU DON'T SAY.'

'In Lane Cove, but I got out early and bought a sheep farm at Inverell.'

'HOW'D THAT GO?'

'Had it forty years and it went backwards on every one.' Lindsay's wife is in the gaming room, being game with a dollar a play on the Oriental Mystic machine.

'I never go in there,' Lindsay says, 'just stand at the door until she sees me. Then we go home.'

Two women walk past our table on their way out. One looks over at a white-haired woman sitting talking to a black-haired girl at a nearby table, maybe her granddaughter. They've been talking and laughing head to head for the fifteen minutes I've been with Lindsay.

'Don't pick up a mop or you'll break it,' says one of the two passing women to the white-haired woman.

Then they're gone.

The white-haired woman looks wonderingly at the backs of the two departing women, then turns to her young companion, who shrugs. Then she swivels around and looks at me.

I shrug.

She shrugs.

Lindsay, in his solemn world of the deaf, hasn't heard a thing.

An attractive woman in a dress of autumnal colours stands in the doorway that leads to the gaming room. She smiles when Lindsay looks over and lifts her right hand, pinky extended.

'Bugger,' says Lindsay softly, 'she wants another drink; now I'll miss M.A.S.H.'

Stoners

Wayne Chance is twenty-eight. He's an old school chum who showed up after an absence of several years. He's a quiet fellow, Chance, and for reasons only they know, none of the dogs barked as he walked by their lockup on his way to the house.

Chance walked up the old wooden steps, dropped his kitbag on the deck, knocked on the open door then walked in. Walked down the hall, through the house to the kitchen then sat at the table waiting for someone to show up.

Pulled out a bag of the makings, rolled a smoke, lit it and sucked back so hard it sparkled. Got up and walked to the fridge, opened it, looked inside, inserted an empty hand and withdrew a full one. Took two steps to the overhead cabinet, opened that and took out two glasses. Came back to the table, set down the glasses, dug a coin out of his fob pocket and jigged the cap off the beer, put that on the table and sat down again. Poured two beers. Ashed his smoke in his hand, waited.

Later that night we were watching television, a leopard leaping at a giraffe's neck, clawing its bloody path back down to the ground as it fell away.

Chance took another smoke outside during the ad break, came back in after five minutes and sat down, looked at the TV.

'What's happening?'

'I flicked the channel.'

Chance nodded at the screen.

'What are we looking at?'

'Some bloke's gone down a Croatian coal mine.'

Chance sat forward.

'Why?'

'Looking for glow worms.'

Good With Equipment

I have a mate name of Dave Rundle, otherwise known as Deadly Dave, Disaster Dave or MX, the *Missile*. We spent a few hours together yesterday with Wayne the cattleman, Les the ex-Navy publican and Jim the Pom. Wives also in attendance, nattering away in the background.

Food and drink on call, nobody in any need.

'One thing about Dave,' I said to the male side of the table, 'he's good with *equipment*, knows what's what and when he's working on one of his cars all the *equipment* is laid out on the bench top, nothing missing.'

I look over at Dave.

'Right, Dave?'

Dave smiles.

'You bastard,' he says.

I continue.

'There was this day when Dave showed up a little late for the early at Mona Vale; we were all out, half way through the before-work session. Lovely waves, midsummer, warm water and everybody happy, even the wave-skis. That's what Dave had for his *equipment* being a goat-boater: a wave-skier. It was stowed in the back of his car.

'Dave does a quick change, grabs his equipment and heads to the water's edge, dumps the ski into the water and then everything stops.'

'Les?' I ask, looking over at him, 'When you're fixing a generator you know what *equipment* you need, right?'

Les nods. He's the wise one.

'A bloke has to know what he's doing.'

Les has an old tattoo on his left upper-arm: the little bloke who inked it up for him in Hong Kong got it wrong and Les has been wearing HMAS *Albatruss* on his arm for over thirty years.

'So?'

This from Jim the Pom. Good value, Jim, but born in the wrong hemisphere.

'Dave's standing knee-deep in water looking over his shoulder.'

'What for?'

'His paddle.'

Dave mutters something unkind about his mate of forty years. His best man.

'It was back in his garage.'

1937

Rebecca

Cormac McCarthy once wrote of hearing a cat shrieking in the night sky – a long, feline howl of fear and rage that passed over his head and continued for some moments into the far hills until the caterwauling was silenced by distance.

An owl had taken the cat.

A similar queer thing happened up here recently. This time it was the woman next door and two dogs. Her skinny red kelpie and the landlord's bulldog.

The bulldog had a big-mouthed clamp on the kelpie's neck and was settling in for the kill. The kelpie was screaming, the woman kneeling over both, shrieking.

'Let him go! Let him GO!'

When we got to her she was wide-eyed and bloodstained with two deep stabs in her forearm; she had separated the dogs and the bulldog was plunging his bloodied mouth into a dish of water nearby.

Rebecca. She lives alone in a one-room shack next door with Bob her kelpie. There was blood on her arms and clothes, mud and dirt on her feet, shins and hands.

Rebecca spent four days in hospital waiting for the infection to clear. Bob barked for her the entire night, every night, until she came home.

Two weeks later Bob got under the boundary fence and was shot by a neighbour.

Max

Max runs the counter at the IGA shop in Lawson Street.

He's about 40. Max collects the cash, swipes the merchandise tag, bags the purchases, counts the change, and sometimes looks up at the no-name nobody on the other side of the counter.

Babes from all over; they speak German, Yiddish, English, Yank, Spanish, Portuguese. Blokes from all over, they speak German, English, Yank, Spanish, Portuguese.

Same as. Babble. Only money talks.

Max sees them come and watches them go. Everyone is watching everyone but nobody catches anybody's eye. This is Byron Bay. No one is a local.

Max checks my litre of Norco milk. I had a mate who used to work in that Johnson Street shed in 1962 for bugger-all an hour. Then he checks my beef sausages. Nobody remembers the stink that wafted down from the meatworks when the north-easter blew into town from Belongil. Then he checks my pack of smokes. Nobody remembers Loose-Leaf and how he dropped nuggets of red dirt and bushy seed up and down Bangalow Road when he went socialising in Lismore.

Lismore women, how they sparkled at the Pier Pub on Saturday night before the music started.

Max has eyes that are bagged up enough for international travel, and when I ask him how Byron is treating him these days he looks up and smiles.

I don't have a rash.

I got goosebumps on that.

The Engine Fitter

Bob P. fitted Cummins engines into the fragile hulls of plastic power boats. A couple of tons of metal and force distributors, hydraulics and electrical connections, drives and gearboxes, differentials and prop shaft connections. Brutal work that broke bones and strained bodies. Engines wedged into spaces with no tolerance for access.

Stinkboats.

Noisy marina queens skippered by the emperors of commerce in 1975. Teetering piles of floating plastic that dared the softest breeze to knock them over.

Bob's son, Davey, an apprentice boatbuilder, aged eighteen. Everybody's friend. Cheerful kid, into everything. Happy to turn the resin gun up out of the hull where he was working when he heard a client walking past, or a manager, and squirt a little of the mix up and over the side of the boat where it settled on hair and shoulders with a frightening permanence.

Vince, labourer, local lad with connections everywhere. Vince always had what was wanted. Vince, sly like a cattledog. Top Price Vince.

Bob took Vince out of the shed one Friday afternoon, walked him out of the lot and into the street, held him firm by the collar with one giant hand and hit him once with the other. Dropped him onto the ground and rolled him into the gutter with his foot.

Midday in Darley street, Mona Vale, all the traffic stopped, people walking out of their factories to see the mayhem – and Bob standing there watching Vince trying to crawl away from further ruin. Bob with his massive hands and oil-stained arms, his clubs.

Then he sacked his son. Walked back into the shed and booted him out. The boy was crying.

Bob talked about it later, his hatred of dope and anyone who dealt with it. I just nodded, agreed, mindful of the rage I had seen. Nobody had told him that his son had bought weed from Vince, but he knew.

Two months later, I had to leave the job in a hurry and Bob was in the office when I came down the stairs packed to go. He looked up and asked if what he'd heard was true, that I was leaving – Yeah mate I said, all done here. Not bloody happy, he replied.

We shook hands. Everybody else was looking the other way.

Davey washed up on the north coast years later, working out of the Brunswick fleet. Still a stoner, hasn't spoken to his dad for thirty years.

The White Mare

He's a squarely built bloke with a boy's quick grin, but his eyes are hard work the way they don't shift when he's talking to you. He just bores them in. Arabs, I hear, like to look away when doing business, or planning things – or just talking. Not Wayne, though. He's high beam today.

He's just come through the gate, seeing as it's open, and scattered everything out of the way coming down the gravel road to the house on his quad bike. The last time he came through like this was to tell us about his white brooding mare. That was last week. She'd been pulled down by dogs and killed, then they ate out her foal, leaving just the head. He had photos.

Since then, he'd hired someone from Coffs Harbour, a dog trapper, to come up and help. Kiwi fellow with no past, no real name, and the pair of them walked through the acres of paddock where the mare was killed, sniffing tree bases.

The trapper had a yellow dingo on a lead and where the beast pulled the two men followed. He let the dog make his mark on a tree and waved Wayne over.

'It stunk so much I near gagged,' said Wayne.

This is where they came at night, scoping out their game from tree to tree. Slipping in and out of the night shadows. Dogtown. Restive horses alive to their movement.

On the first day, Wayne cleared the paddock of stock and the Kiwi laid 50 snap-jaw dog traps. Big steel snapping bastards. Even when their paws are crushed the dogs don't make any noise, and given enough time they chew off the trapped leg and limp away.

I'm looking at my neighbour here, he hasn't got off the bike, he's wearing a scoped Ruger77 on his shoulder and his smile couldn't be any wider.

'Two,' he says, 'last night.'

'How big?'

'Dunno, haven't seen 'em yet, waiting on the Kiwi to tell me where they are.'

The trapper had been out early and had rung in the score on his mobile.

Later, I watch Wayne drag one of the dead dogs across the field. He'd tied it behind his quaddy on a long piece of rope and was bouncing it off every rock he could find.

Good karma, reckoned Wayne, not that he needed any.

Fitzy

Did I tell you about Fitzy?

Years ago, a bloke travelled up to Mudgee Region on some errand or other for the boss. A stocktake, or a stock audit, or a forensic look at the cash accounting which meant tension for the clerk lifting a few hundred here and there from payables. Paying relatives for babysitting the children she never wanted, or for weekends down the road with just another fellow in a motel wallpapered with promises.

Gulgong's three pubs were locked tight against the weather and Jeff Fenech on the bill.

How we all loved watching that tough little fighter. Who of you have ever picked a fight with a man who never stops coming?

The fire was banked up, the bar was crowded, the publican was splashing rum about and we were sat with Fitzy at a table by the wall.

In those days, Gulgong had a home run by the Salvos for the care and redemption of the unfortunates they netted in their sweeps of Sydney's streets. Men with eyes like raspberry jelly, starving old husks from wars, peace and suburban famine; like Fitzy, stuck in here waiting for the fight, sitting next to me and the good lady. A lifetime of hard living written all over him, his conversation a litany of errors.

Fenech rumbled away above us and the bar noise swelled and receded as the rounds checked by and by then Fitzy wanted to know what catching waves was like, standing up on moving water and sliding away and down on the warm blue face of a long swell bending around a Queensland sandspit.

Fitzy, lost to all his family, just another relic of manhood, appropriated to a bed in some windy dormitory well in advance of his final day, exorcised by the well-meant prayers and actions of saintly men and here we sit, drinks in hand, hooting as Fenech punched his opponent to the canvas for the second time.

Fitzy didn't say how he had got away from the confines of the home, just a wink as he punched me lightly on the arm. 'Getting back in half-shot might be a worry,' he said.

He was wearing a fox skin vest, part furried up and part bald, something he'd killed, skinned and cured in his professional days, and he gave it to me.

That was forty-five years ago.

Part Seven
Other Lives

Home

Digging into a dumped load of shredded camphor laurel, a young woman by the side of the road. Spading up clumps of rotting waste into a wheelbarrow. Behind her in the gloom of the forest is a caravan. She has a garden.

Home, almost overcome by the stately weeds that claim preponderance after weeks of monsoon rain. She has a shallow plot of tomatoes and peas, a couple of cannabis plants turned hermaphrodite, useless, and two small children scampering about barefoot in a forest of brown snakes and black leeches.

Something scrabbles over the caravan roof at night. Sometimes a car travels by late, and they stop and turn around on the road by her home, squirting rock and dirt into the air. She leaps awake, listening for a car door. There is never a light here at night, but still they come. A bottle fizzing through the air, they howl and depart. Their car growling away and into the hills.

Wild dogs are silent, except for faint rustlings as they slide through the weeds and beneath the caravan floor Sometimes a whimper as a young dog is taught stealth.

She is awake.

Three hundred and Thirty-One Days

December 2016

Bunnings, Lismore, out the back in the garden section. I'm wandering the rows of tomato seedlings looking for the same sweet little babies I bought last year. When I turned around to go back here's this big fellow a yard away, he's holding two tomato seedlings, one in each hand.

'G'day,' he says.

Unshaven, six foot three, one hundred kilogrammes. Clear eyes.

'How you going?' I say.

'Pretty good, last year the doctor said I only had three months to live.'

He held up one of the tomato seedlings.

'So I bought a couple of these and planted them.'

'Any good?'

'I had one a day for three hundred and thirty-one days, now I'm back for more.'

Two Men

He had injected his irises with an iridescent deep green marble, leaving the pupils looking like shining black beetles. He glanced at me.

His legs – he was wearing shorts – were inked solid and his arms dense with colour. The artwork crept from beneath his shirt to his chin. His face was tattooed with scarlet geometric patterns. A triangle under one eye, a rectangle on one cheek, red strips on his forehead. Dots and blots.

Metal stapled into his ears, nose, tongue and lips.

A man in there, somewhere.

'Excuse me.'

We were standing at the window of a Strand Arcade jewellery shop in Sydney.

'How many hundreds of hours of pain did it take to have all that done to you?'

He looked back to the window display, the emeralds and opals, the aquamarines and diamonds.
The street cleaner stopped his collecting, rested his broom against the cart and looked about at the crowds

who wandered the Pitt Street Mall. Underneath their feet were hundreds of cigarette butts, thousands of leaves from the over-shadowing plane trees, litter.

He wore an orange council jacket, peaked cap and sunglasses. He was about forty. Lean, burnt dark by the sun on his neck and forearms. I walked over.

'How long have you been doing this?'

He looked away, at the people all around us.

'This is me first day.'

A long-limbed woman wearing chiffon and bathed in Estee Lauder walked by.

'… and the last.'

Ronnie

Ronnie sidled over to the table wearing a whiskery half-smile with two forks and one knife in his left hand. His right held a can of fresh-opened beer. Fizzed up and leaking onto his shoes.

A little later he passed by once more, this time with the other knife.

Then he stood some small way off, just within speaking distance, looking to the river and grizzling with his free hand at the white whiskers that powdered his veiny red face.

Preoccupied with his thirst.

A mob of kookaburras voiced a crescendo from across the water and Ronnie looked over at our table, his eyes lighting upon the unopened bottle of ten-dollar sparkling wine standing there.

In a moment he was gone and then was back with a corkscrew, then again with a ceramic wine cooler which was too small.

This gave him some pause and he stepped back a little and consulted his beer.

The second story verandah that wrapped around the two sides of the riverside kiosk had about ten small tables and only one other was occupied.

Ronnie was wearing a uniform of sorts and his shoulder tabs read 'Riverhire'.

From time to time he retired to the bar where his clipboards and papers were arranged, and he busily notated various facts and notions, all the while conversing confidentially into a small mobile phone kept precious by his ear.

A precocious group of four Noisy Minors swooped into the verandah and distributed themselves amongst the rafters and decorative lanyards.

'I don't work here you know,' offered Ronnie from close by and without warning. He was holding a battered metal cooler for the wine

'I just like to help the lass when she's on her own.' He had refreshed his drink.

'I live up the hill, you know, on me own, mostly go fishing. Been a single bloke all me life.'

He stayed close by. He drank. His smile flickered on and off.

'Young bloke up here blew up a swimmin' pool the other day you know. Wouldn't credit it.'

He had put the wine bottle into the cooler. It was big enough for a magnum.

'You'll want a couple of glasses for that now, won't you?' – and away he went again.

A minor flew down onto the table and scoped it for food. His brother hung upside down from a lanyard tied around the verandah rail and they both called and were back-called from their family of half-dozen or so who scavenged around a triple row of dories stacked by the boat ramp. A bearded crow sat in a tall eucalypt and cursed everyone and everything.

'Sparklers.' Ronnie placed two glasses on the tablecloth.

'He made the bomb from sparklers, got 'em at the local paper shop. Grounded the powder off 'em all, jammed the stuff into a coke bottle, stuck in a wick, laid it alongside the pool wall. Lit it. Scarpered. Boom!

Ronnie stood back and tested the level of his new beer.

'Everyone knows who done it.'

David came by later. He was the yacht club's caretaker. It said so on his teeshirt: David – Caretaker – Y*acht Club*.

The silver earring added little allure to his hard-used face. Neck and head equally squat. His small nose many times broken, thick arms thickly haired, muscular legs chunked into steel caps. Watchful eyes, faded tattoos, antique and faint and half-hidden underneath his rolled shirtsleeves. Women self-engraved while at leisure.

'Ten per cent would be arseholes, the rest are okay.'

This in answer to a question nobody would think of asking.

He was addressing the membership ledgers while sat at an adjoining table, inviting no response. Drinking.

Ronnie put his fresh beer down and cleared the table, a little unsteady now as he gathered the crockery. He took the plates and his beer away.

'Good little fisherman, that bloke,' said David. 'Could hook a jewy as big as a young shark, fifty, seventy pound.'

He nodded at the door Ronnie had disappeared into.

'Likes a touch of the drink a little too much these days. That's one of his boats over there.'

He pointed at a small cabin-topped motorboat moored fifty feet away. Listing to portside, green-bellied. Heavy in the water.

'Been here for thirty-five years, he reckons, and I don't doubt it.'

He slowly eased himself up from the table and walked away.

'See youse around,' he said.

Two tourists in khaki shorts and shirts were standing on a pontoon having their picture taken by a third. The woman was holding a fork in the air and they were both laughing. Ronnie, newly refreshed, stood at the railing looking down at the tableau. He rubbed his chin, consulted his beer, and wandered over as we rose from our table.

'Have a drink before you go?'

We walked into the kiosk and he asked the lass for another round. She passed over three cans and gave Ronnie his chit to sign. Looking down at it he laughed and gestured for me to come over. The docket dated today and noted 'Ronnie' had eighteen strokes marked on it. Eighteen cans.

'Doesn't include the couple after breakfast out of the fridge either,' he chuckled. 'Been on a slab a day for about five years.'

A little later he waved us off.

'Hope the little bastard hasn't blown up yer car.'

We passed by the security-fenced compound that contained a hillside of boulders and forest and in the gloom we saw David standing there, nearly hidden among the tall eucalyptus; he was gazing through the bars of their long shadows and at the glittering reach of river water beyond.

Reunion

He'd been optimistic about the night after someone had improbably sought him out and included him in the roll call. A list of names accompanied the invitation. Old friends.

Old enemies.

Everybody was asked to meet in the main bar of the Bondi Diggers early evening and then continue upstairs to the old function room for the main events.

He arrived alone and moved straight to a corner of the bar where he slowly scanned the faces of the other men in the room. Features fattened beyond recognition by wealth or success, or whittled by poor health or addiction, or hidden behind some guilt that makes an old friend a stranger. Some had brought their wives, women whose faces were the tide table of their husband's affairs.

Some of the old cliques needed little reviving and like a pack of dogs they still had a sensitive nose for an outsider. He could hear their laughter. There was no special old friend because there was no special young friend forty-five years ago: and groups of four had no room for a fifth, and after five drinks he soured up.

The function room had not been used for years and with all the furniture gone and the fittings stripped it offered no welcome to the thirty or so who bothered to move up from the downstairs bar when they were called. They stood about in the quiet, smothered by the sobering gloom.

Somebody found a microphone, another his guitar and a couple of young women began dancing together. Sounds of laughter drifted in from a balcony that looked out over the darkened beach and a harsh bar light spilled onto the features of the men waiting on their drinks. They looked like mourners.

He arrived home much later than she expected and full of whiskey. The teeshirt and cap he'd been given to commemorate the reunion were crumpled and sodden with beer so she threw them out without hesitation. He would have little recollection of any of it by morning, his memory flickering between fiction and reality.

A few years ago, she had found herself picking through the old surfing magazines that he'd collected as a young surfer, hoping to find a picture of him – her good-looking man.

And there he was, a boy sitting alone on a low headland at the Pass in 1964, watching the long waves sweep past.

Roundarm, Trepiditious and Fungry

Eric 'Roundarm' Pierce lives in a modest manor a block or two north of Ettalong town centre.

His tidy garden necklaces the four asbestos walls and tin roof that shield him from rain and heat, and by day and by night the deadly motes drift into his food, into his bed, and into his gaping mouth as he lies asleep.

Not alone though, Eric with his two dogs: Trepiditious the Jack Russell and Fungry the Mixed.

Eric is a big man with long broad arms and the shoulders of a road worker and he wanders up and down the beach from time to time with Trep and Fungry, plus a couple of tennis balls and an old wooden racquet that washed up on Lobster Beach in 1948.

His old dad found the racquet floating in from Box Head during the May '48 cyclone swell.

There was an old photo on the wall of a Pearl Beach restaurant that showed a succession of fifteen-foot swells stacking up past the northern point and travelling diagonally past a white-watered Pearl Beach and down into the long sands of Ocean Beach a couple of days after the cyclone passed. Right into the face of an out of season north westerly.

You can tell the conditions by the blownback mist from the top of the sets and the smiles on the faces of the three surfers in the foreground of the photo: Eric's dad; Jimmy Longduds from an Aboriginal camp by Kourung Gourung; and Ken from Avalon. Boys then, black-backed from exposure to the sun and wind, all squared up in the shoulders from paddling their big boards.

Smiling.

Eric wanders up the beach to the jetty on some days, with his couple of dogs, his racquet and tennis balls.

Trep's ball is hit into the shallows because the little Jack Russell is old now and near blinded by bindii. Fungry though is a different dog. Half border collie with a solid squirt of working kelpie.

Eric stands on the beach and nods the dog onto the jetty, then slams the ball out into deep water. Fung streaks down the old boards and inches from the jetty edge he launches himself, hitting the water about twenty feet from the pylons.

WHOOMPF!

There would have been about thirty travellers on the top deck of the 9.30 this morning, all heading to Palm Beach for a million reasons.

There must have been 60 surfers out at Avalon today.

A bloke I've known for 30 years walked past me and looked the other way.

Someone screams around here every other night about 2am.

Always the same word.

Waiting for a Takeaway

This bloke.

He's sitting at an outside table at the Doma cafe with about six friends. He's maybe under thirty, fully presentable, the girls at the table too lovely to look at. I'm inside waiting for lunch, their car is out the front with about eight boards on the roof. I'm watching him because he's sitting at the head of the table waving his arms about to draw his friends' attention to what he's saying.

Big laugher. Nice teeth. *Showboat.*

Food comes and he begins to eat, forgoing further conversation with the lovely at his side, the long *brown*-legged lovely. If only she were a painting.

Showboat consumed his lunch over seven quick innings.

Total time at the crease: eight minutes and thirty seconds.

These innings were a count of the number of times Showboat's mouth opened to accommodate an incoming load while still being occupied with the previous deposit.

Load and eat. Re-load and eat. Re-load and eat. When he stopped to chat or wipe his mouth, I stopped counting, committed his score to memory and waited for the next innings.

Innings one: 10

Innings two: 10

Before leaving, I asked one of the girls if I could have a scrap of paper.

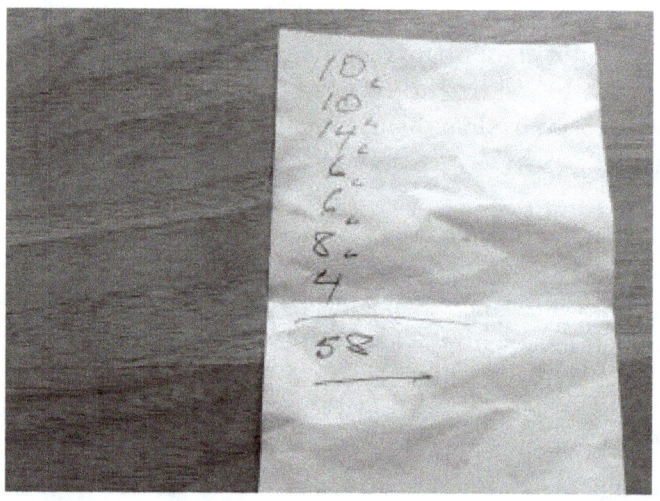

One Japanese-style burger with a side dish of red chilli downed in fifty-eight hits. Consecutive innings of ten, then a fourteen, two sixes, an eight and finishing with a four.

Showboat sits back, wipes his face on his collar and raises a hand to his mouth to deal with the rising gastronomical consequences. A sheen of perspiration has appeared on his brow. His forehead is knuckling.

Later on, I told Al.

'What?' he says. 'You've got nothing better to do?'

I shrug, open my hands.

'I was waiting for a takeaway.'

The Kelpie

Federal – NSW postcode 2480 – is a right-hand turn coming up from Binna Burra or a left coming down from Lismore. It has one general store, one sushi café, a caravan selling Mediterranean food and one retail coffee maker. Most of the buildings lean. An old Queensland-style homestead sits fenced and abandoned on a vacant lot across the road.

I'm watching a red kelpie set loose among the café's outside tables; his only interests are the small plastic hose lug he carries around with him and the foot he has just placed it by. The foot belongs to a woman too busy on her phone to notice the large red dog staring fixedly at her toes. Red is a statue.

I flick my fingers and Red looks up at me, a quick glance, then back to the foot.

The temperature is over 30 degrees, no wind, humid.

A party of three walk in, one is wearing something Arabic: a shawl big enough to cover her head and fall to her waist where she has gathered it in. Another is a broad-shouldered man wearing white trousers and a white singlet, the third a young woman wearing far too little. A man can only look away.

Red inches towards his lug, touches it with his nose and moves it a centimetre closer to the woman's foot. He is motionless but for a small tremor that ripples through him every time she moves a toe.

She's still talking.

I flick my fingers again.

Another glance from Red, then back to the woman's foot.

She's still talking.

One of the Japanese girls who works in the café, Ayame, told me last week she had come to Australia to look for a man. Then she gave a grin cheeky enough for me to believe her.

Sota is on the griddle most days. We compare shirts from time to time. I get mine at Tommy Bahamas in the Bay and Sota buys his at the Ballina Vinnies shop. He paid five dollars for the one he's got on today and it's quality.

The lady on the phone gets up from her seat, treads on Red's lug and stands a little way off, still talking. Red bites up his lug and follows her, lays it down by her foot. Stares at her toes.

I flick. Red looks up at me.

Then back to the foot.

Bob McTavish and a party of four roll up. I haven't seen that old boy since Warren Cornish's funeral. We catch each other's eye and Bob sits his friends down and comes over for a chat. Old times. This fellow and that fellow, who's still breathing and who isn't. His books, my books. Bob looks like he could live for another fifty years and he's going to be bandy for all of them.

At my age it's optimism to say see you later to a good man.

The phone lady comes back to her table, they all pack up and leave. Red picks up his lug and walks over to a bench where two men are sitting drinking coffee, tradesmen, their pick-up outside. Red places his lug by the foot of the biggest then goes into his watching routine again.

As I walk past them on the way out, I stop and ask the big bloke if he could do me a favour. Gesture at Red and his lug down there.

'You want to give that thing a nudge, mate? He needs the work.'

Another Life

The old man driving the yellow kombi followed me to the property gate and I turned to look at him as he drove by. We might have known each other in another life, old men are hard to recognise behind their beards.

The woman was still walking on the side of the road, this time coming towards me: the same woman in black with a black dog, walking through the knee-high grasses that flower and spread by the roadside. Not many homes out here in the hills, and what there are have long approaches.

She didn't look up as I passed, only a man does that, sometimes. She was dressed in slacks and a blouse. A wide-brimmed black hat, tied with a red ribbon.

The dog was tethered to her hand with a leather strap, a red ribbon tied to its collar. Listening *at* the cars, the few that passed them by.

The lower half of her face was porcelain, unblemished, apparent in the second it took to pass. Red lipstick, pale skin.

Eyes downcast.

Walking, on.

Marcus came by: he was out walking, he said, at his place – to the shade-house where two sleek, black birds are hunting the wren chicks.

Marcus wears boots and jeans, and when he goes about at this time of year he carries a Dutch hoe. He is partial to keeping it clean and sharp, snakes for the use of:

One day he trod on one, clanked down about half way along its glistening brown length. The snake whipped up and around and wasted its poison on boot leather before Marcus got the blade down onto its neck and sawed it into two parts. Well, not so much *saw*, the Dutch hoe is a straight blade, but bear down, and cut through, using the edges.

The head still bites, he said, you can watch, or stamp the life out of it.

Marcus used to wait tables at a little Italian restaurant in Five Dock. He never told anyone why he left in the middle of service. The three men who arrived that night didn't order then came back looking for him twice more.

Part Eight
Surviving

An Income

The child Yukio S survived the titanic waves of radiation that cleansed his neighbourhood after the American bomb swept Hiroshima away.

His mother's body was photographed some six months later by the Americans; it was imprinted faintly on the remnant wall of the small tailor's shop that had for years provided an income for her small family while Yukio's father tended to the Allied prisoners of war building the Burma Railway.

She wore floral that last day; see her opalescent head combs riven into the rough plaster of the ruined wall of the bedroom she shared with Yukio and his sister.

Yukio S lives in Torquay these days and although unable to either hear or speak he has built up a niche market in miniature Japanese typhoon gardens.

Yukio uses three grades of crushed Queensland marble, large porous granite boulders and a lifetime of bonsai culture to create passive islands in the midst of typhoon swells.

He subjects the granite to five years of nitrogen enhanced drip condensation to build up a deep mossy base, thick enough to support a forest of miniature radiata on the rock's crest.

He sets the boulder central in a sea of fine marble leavings, not unlike a mountaintop breaching the sea, and fashions the majestic and symmetrical lines of storm surf surrounding the breach in carefully arrayed lines of finer crushed marble, all set permanently in clear resin.

The individual gardens are mounted on an eight-inch teak base and are relatively portable. They suit small inner-city dwellings, childless couples.

The melancholy among us.

Prices vary.

Anzac Day

Every three months we come to town, this time it was Anzac Day.

I used to watch my father march from the Westin side of George Street. The Boss. That was the only time he liked to walk, other than when he was playing golf. He was an artist on the course. He used to reckon I was a bullshit artist off it.

It's about midday in the city and the bands are coming back along Elizabeth Street, all done with playing. Some rag-tag little pickles of kids toting heavy kettle drums and flagpoles among the larger private school pipe bands. There's one in the hotel restaurant; they've left their bearskins and drums, pipes and flutes stacked against the walls while they scoff a Sheraton buffet. Fifty or so, all men. Hairy Scots with Australian accents.

Before they leave for the bus to take them home, they assemble on the lobby stairs and play. Twenty pipes, six drums. Battle pipes to raise all the hairs on both your arms.

The army officer was standing on the same steps an hour later. His cap *on*, two rows of ribbons on the left breast of his khaki uniform. The body under his leather-cinched uniform square about the shoulders and hard about the waist.

'Excuse me.'

The soldier looks down at the older man, standing a step below him.

'Yes?'

'I promised my father every Anzac Day I'd find a soldier and shake his hand. He was a fighter pilot. Dead now.'

The soldier nods, and takes the older man's extended hand.

Anthem

*A*ustralians let us all rejoice
The Appin Massacre
The Bathurst Massacre
The Waterloo Creek Massacre
The Myall Creek Massacre

For we are young and free;

The Gwydir River War
The Murrumbidgee Wiradjuri Wars
The Rufus River Massacre

We've golden soil and wealth for toil;

The Evans Head Massacre
The Nyngan Massacre
The Risdon Cove Massacre

Our home is girt by sea;

The Cape Grim Massacre
The Van Diemens Land Genocide
The Convincing Grounds Massacre

Our land abounds in nature's gifts of beauty rich and rare;

The Faithful Massacre
The Wangaratta Massacre
The Campapsi Plains Massacre
The Murdering Gully Massacre

In history's page, let every stage Advance Australia Fair.

The Gippsland Massacre
The Warrigal Creek Massacre
The Cape Otway Massacre
The Hospital Creek Massacre
The Butchers Tree Massacre

In joyful strains then let us sing,

The Fremantle Massacre
The Battle of Pinjara.
The Lake Minimup Massacre
The La Grange Expedition Massacre

Advance Australia Fair.

The Flying Foam Massacre
The Halls Creek Massacre
The Kimberley Killing Times.
The Avenue Range Station Massacre

Beneath our radiant Southern Cross We'll toil with hearts and hands;

The Whiteside Poisoning
The Kilcoy Poisoning
The Upper Burnett Massacre
The Balonne Massacre

The Condamine Killings

To make this Commonwealth of ours Renowned of all the lands;

The Paddy Island Massacre
The Massacre of the Yeeman Tribe.
The Water View Massacre
The Medway ranges Massacre

For those who've come across the seas We've boundless plains to share;

The Goulbolba Massacre
The Bowen River Disappearances
The Mistake Creek Massacre
The Battle Camp Massacre
The Blackfellows Creek Massacre
The Cook District Massacre
The Welwyn Range Massacre

With courage let us all combine

The Cape Bedford Massacre
The Battle Mountain Massacre
The Diamantina River Massacre
The Speewah Massacre
The Barrow Creek Massacre
The Florida Station Massacre
The Canning Stock Route Killings
The Bedford Downs Poisoning

To Advance Australia Fair.

The Forrest River Massacre
The Bentinck Island Massacres
The Coniston Massacre

In joyful strains then let us sing,

Advance Australia Fair.

What We Might Wish For, for Christmas, for the Old Boys

a little peace and quiet
an empty sky
a diary of the past
two lanes from sydney to angourie
screw-down racks
balsa shavings
a hat like bob cooper's
front row at a severson movie
a nod from bob evans
ten boards on one car roof
a weekend at the farm
flicking a bottle cap at a traffic cop
copping a smile from a wollongong girl
a shirt like bob coopers.
front row at the patch on saturday afternoon
nobody out at wategos
nobody out at granite

a lismore girl

a chinese feed at bondi junction

watching bondi united

empty north av in a nor'wester

billy thorpe at surf city –

getting past the bouncer at tabu in the cross

watching big men fight at the sheaf

watching farrelly

hating nat, watching nat, loving nat beat the yanks

owning byron

tomato fights at bulli pass

broken head and watermelons

watching peterson

dole-bludging with integrity

fighting Q'landers

loving Q'landers

sleeping in the crescent shed

nobody out at tea tree

hearing midget laugh

bingo at brunswick

the goldie beer gardens

12 hours to the tweed

currumbin … 6' … sweeping to the beach

six to a van at conjola

watching a yank try to roll a tight number

eight in a circle and ten joints on the circuit

watching weather report at the hordern pav

walking up bondi road

drinking at the astra

playing street rugby

surviving

Also by Peter Bowes

Bloodlines

His short vignettes in Bloodlines are visceral, teeth rattling, funny and even true, and they stretch from then to now and this horizon to that, from the poetic to the poignant to the hilarious. ~ Sean Doherty author of *My Brother's Keeper* and *MP: The Life of Michael Peterson* published by HarperCollins.

Lineage

The second in Peter Bowes' 'Bloodlines' trilogy.

To open the pages of a book by Peter Bowes is to enter a quintessentially Australian world, but one that is also universal. We all know these people, see them on the streets, meet them, avoid them, want to know more about them.

The Bookmaker from Rabaul

A meticulously researched fictionalised account of the Somerton Man mystery. Includes an afterword detailing the known facts of the case.

Opening pages of
The Bookmaker from Rabaul

Is This the Man?

DS Leane was asking a question.

He spoke again.

'Do you know this man?'

The detectives had dusty shoes and the one called Brown a ragged edge to one of his trouser cuffs.

'No.'

'Would you please look at the bust? Is this man Alfred Baxter?'

'No.'

Leane exchanged glances with Canney.

'Mrs Beecham?'

Tangiers, 1938

They were bare-chested. The slighter, bespectacled man's face had burnt a sharp red in the Moroccan sun; a wide-brimmed black hat protected his taller companion.

Both men were looking over the hotel parapet down onto the Grand Socco where a procession of donkeys was being led through the crowds to the dockside warehouses, all double-loaded with hessian bags of kief brought down from the Atlas Mountains overnight and destined for Spain.

A young girl from a café across the square brought them a small plate of hashish galletas and a stone pot of cream with their coffee. She had surprised them on the first morning when she pushed aside the curtain that served as a door and brought her tray into the rooftop bedroom they shared, and from that day the Englishman called her Mata Hari because she knew their secrets.

The windless morning promised another hot day.

'The war will change everything.'

Pym gestured at the Mediterranean's distant, tranquil surface.

'This …'

He turned to his companion, who had just picked up one of the flat biscuits and split it with his thumbnail.

'Us.'

Seed

Moscow, 1941

The lecturer had an Albanian name: Otto Troseth … Trozyth? He mentioned it as the six recruits settled into their seats in the small windowless classroom, young men and women, pale from their long weeks of learning the operational intricacies of a dozen different cipher machines. Trozyth wished them good afternoon. The two women smiled at him, the men remained impassive.

He held up a small soft-covered book and wondered, as he did with all his classes, how many of them had ever finished a book they didn't have to read.

'This book contains seventy-five quatrains, seven to nine words per line, twenty-five to thirty letters on each line.'

Otto opened the lid of his desk, took out another five copies and walked around distributing them.

'In each book you will find a sheet of paper with two typed stanzas.'

He waited until everybody had found and read them.

I, a fugitive caravanserai,
crept silently east.

That yellow, departed hand,
be with me again.
Thou seed.

'If I were to write a covert message using this book, wherein I described my present situation, my method of travel and destination, would you agree that the first verse is sufficient?'

No one spoke.

'Well? Somebody speak up please.'

One of the women looked around before slowly raising her hand.

'Yes?'

'I am a fugitive. I am coming east.'

'What is your name?'

'Yana.'

'What else do you know of your fugitive, Yana?'
The young woman bent her head and read the verse again, then spoke without looking up.

'He is travelling overland under forged identification papers, perhaps by train. Nobody knows where he has gone.'

Otto took a piece of chalk from his pocket and turned to the blackboard.

'Which words did you use to arrive at those considerations, Yana?'

'I. Fugitive. Caravanserai. Crept. Silently. East.'

Otto wrote the six words on the board.

'Explain how the word crept metamorphoses into forged identification to the class, all of whom seem to be struck dumb.'

Otto had little time for the thick-minded and wasted no effort with them. He turned and looked at the young woman.

'Forged identification. How did that come into being, Yana?'

'Anyone who travels with proper papers does so openly; it is another matter for someone on forged papers.'

Otto smiled

'They creep from place to place?'

'Yes, sir, that is my interpretation.'

'Then I hope you never have to travel under such a burden. Why don't his superiors know of his movements?'

'He has kept silent.'

Trozyth looked over at the other students until one met his glance and raised his hand.

'Yes?'

'I am familiar with the book, but not those lines.'

'Your name?'

'Oskar.'

Otto faced the board and chalked a line of characters, speaking as he wrote.

LIV 1 1 XXIV 3 1 XXXV 1 7 XVI 1 5

'There are enough words in the *Rubaiyat* to satisfy any message.'

He turned around, placed the chalk on his desk and looked at each student in turn; he had no doubt some would fall asleep if he allowed it.

'Oskar, what is the fifth word on the first line of verse sixteen in the book you have on your desk?'

Oskar picked up the book and flicked through the pages.

'Caravanserai.'

'What does the word represent, now that Yana has broken the code?'

Oskar and Yana exchanged a quick glance.

'An agent, in flight.'

Otto looked over at Yana.

'What of the second stanza?'

'It is a response: I will be where we last met. All is well.'

'Where will they meet?'

'Hong Kong, China.'

'China?'

'They are the yellow people.'

'All is well?'

'Seed.'

She was worth all the hundreds who passed through his classes.

'What if all is not well?'

'There would be no seed.'

Otto allowed a small triumphal surge to quicken his blood before looking away from the girl's face and back at the class.

'Perhaps you could explain?'
'A seed grows; its absence means nothing will come of a meeting.'

Exodus

Hong Kong, 1941

The correspondent had arrived in Hong Kong with orders to retrieve a package from the Russian legation's safety room, now being emptied. It was to have been picked up and taken to Australia by a regular courier but the recent and rapid course of the war had hurried the exodus from the island. The courier had abandoned the city and an orderly search of his rooms took fifteen minutes to come up with nothing. He had gone.

The correspondent knew where to go and was in and out of the building quickly. His escape from the colony now depended on a merchant steamer, the *Cycle*, docked a few miles east and no doubt anxious to be away from the air battles drifting over the city. The roads along the waterfront were choked with emigrants and expatriates, the footpaths piled with abandoned possessions, the air steaming with panic. The Japanese were already in Kowloon, almost at the edge of Victoria Harbour, and the only escape from Hong Kong Island was by boat.

George Lorrimer had been sitting on two stacked wooden crates behind the kitchen window of an empty Hong Kong office suite for two days. He was uncomfortable and had no electricity to boil water for the coffee he kept in a tin in his camera case. Perch jobs, he hated them.

This was not the first time Frank Delaney had given him the key to these rooms. They were across the road from the Russian legation and the cigarette butts he'd ground onto the floor earlier in the year were still there, as were the exposed nail heads on the crates and the cockroach husks in the cupboards.

When he slid open the window above the sink, the uproarious clamour of engines and voices from the street filled the room. The roads were chaotic, the noise of the traffic pierced by the continual wailing of older Chinese women among the crowds, lamenting their doomed right to live in Hong Kong: the Jewel. The Japanese would be cruel and brutal and here in days.

Lorrimer rested his camera on the work surface to his left together with his notepad and pencil. The enamel sink, directly beneath his chin, had a blackened and ungated cavity at its centre and at times a low grumble came from its depths, as if from some internal shifting of organs, issuing soft gusts of foul wet air into his face as he watched the doorway across the street.

He shook three Lucky Strike cigarettes out of his packet and arranged them next to his camera, then took a silver Zippo lighter from his trouser pocket and laid it alongside them. Three cigarettes for a three-hour shift before a break outside in fresher air.

A noise in the corridor and Lorrimer turned to see a shadow pass beneath the door.

He got up from his seat and quietly crossed the room, opened the door and stepped out into a deserted hallway that stretched fifty feet one way and fifty feet the other. He looked to his left and right then came back inside, closed and locked the door, resumed his seat, took up his first cigarette, lit it, put the lighter back into his pocket, picked up his camera and focused it on the legation entrance.

'Who do you want?' he had asked Delaney. 'They'll be coming in and out like it's a Woolworths store.'

'Anyone with a white face.'

On the second day, Lorrimer saw two men inside the lobby exchanging a package before they separated and left the building.

Both were wearing hats; one slightly built, dressed in suit and tie and wearing glasses, the other broad-shouldered and squat; a seaman, wearing a pea-jacket, dungarees and heavy boots.

He weighed it up: follow the package, or the man who had sent it on its way.

Lorrimer was used to the crowded Hong Kong streets and sometimes tried his hand at trailing a local man who looked to be in a hurry. But following one black-crowned head into these confounding mazes of alleyways and streets had proved impossible; at times he had to stop, stranded and directionless in the dark and almost subterranean depths of the city, among a silent people who looked at him without overt curiosity, assuming the oriental stillness of temple cats to watch him until he was gone.

He skirted the crowded footpaths by walking in the gutter and looked for a man wearing a hat in a crowd of hatless Chinese. One small boy coming towards him slipped away from his mother's hand, walked onto the road in front of Lorrimer and stopped to stare at him. Lorrimer stepped around the child and was startled by the impatient bleat of a car horn; he turned to watch a silver chauffeur-driven Rolls-Royce pass slowly by with two women in the back seat, one smoking, both wearing hats. One of the women turned her head to look at Lorrimer as he stood in the gutter on the other side of her window. She glanced up into his eyes from beneath the brim of her hat.

Two blocks on he had him. One block further and Lorrimer watched as Oskar Rostov walked to a dockside gate, produced a piece of paper and handed it to a uniformed officer who stamped it, passed it back and let him through.

Rostov walked in the direction of three steamers tied bow to stern along the wooden dock, all with their gangways down, crowded with lines of slowly climbing evacuees. Small groups stood about the dockside, families, some in tears as they embraced each other.

Rostov moved through them quickly; oblivious to the women's despair as they held their husbands; the men were certain to be imprisoned for the duration of the war after giving up their berths to allow more women and children to flee.

Lorrimer passed through the gate using one of Delaney's police dockets and watched Rostov join a gangway that led to the upper deck of the *Cycle*. He was the only passenger without a suitcase.

Bennison Books

Bennison Books has four imprints:

Contemporary Classics
Great writing from new authors

Non-Fiction
Interesting and useful works written by experts

People's Classics
Handpicked golden oldies by favourite and forgotten authors

Poetic Licence
Poetry and poetic works

Bennison Books is named after Ronald Bennison,
an aptly named blessing.

Bennisonbooks.com

www.ingramcontent.com/pod-product-compliance
Lightning Source LLC
Chambersburg PA
CBHW060812120626
46557CB00001B/182